SECRETS OF THE SCEPTER

UNICORNS OF BALINOR

SECRETS OF THE SCEPTER

MARY STANTON

AN
APPLE
PAPERBACK

SCHOLASTIC INC.
New York Toronto London Auckland Sydney
Mexico City New Delhi Hong Kong

Cover illustration by D. Craig

ISBN 0-439-12048-9

12 11 10 9 8 7 6 5 4 3 2 1   0 1 2 3 4 5/0

Printed in the U.S.A.   40
First Scholastic printing, January 2000

For Josephine and Nicholas DiChario

SECRETS OF THE SCEPTER

1

Atalanta, the Dreamspeaker, stood proud and happy in the Celestial Valley. The Celestial unicorn's violet coat glowed brightly in the morning. The sunlight glinted off her crystal horn and threw a dazzling prism of color across the waters of the Watching Pool. Behind her, the emerald meadows of the Celestial Valley spread out like the train of a velvet dress.

Victory! And all because of Princess Arianna and her Bonded unicorn, the Sunchaser! Atalanta's silvery mane and tail blew exultantly in the gentle breeze. She turned to view her brothers and sisters. The unicorns of the Celestial Valley herd grazed peacefully on the lush grass by the Imperial River.

From his cave on the side of the Eastern Ridge, Numinor, the Golden One, watched over his herd. The Crystal Arch glimmered brightly over them all, one end reaching toward the sky, where the One Who Rules lived, the other leading down to Balinor and the humans the Celestial Valley herd was destined to guard for all time.

Victory! Atalanta whinnied her joy again. Arianna and the Sunchaser had returned the magical Indigo Star to its rightful place in Blue Mountain. The Princess and her unicorn had saved the colors of the blue band and the other unicorn colors in the Celestial Valley. Now there was a chance to overthrow the evil Shifter and bring peace to the humans and animals below the Celestial Valley!

Atalanta approached the Watching Pool with light, graceful steps. The Deep Magic gave her two ways of monitoring the humans and animals she guarded. The first was in dreams, when Atalanta walked the Path of the Moon to visit those below as they slept. The second was through the Watching Pool, where Atalanta could see into the lives of both those who were good and evil.

She would use the Watching Pool now. She splashed one forefoot gently in the water. The Watching Pool was beautiful. There was nothing like it in all the worlds. Perfectly round, the pool was made of amethyst rock, which reflected sunset-colored shadows into the water. Atalanta dipped her crystal horn into the water three times. Her voice was low and musical. "I call on the Princess Arianna and her unicorn, the Sunchaser."

The waters spun gently. And in the depths, a

vision formed. Blue Mountain rose high and towered in the sky. The oldest, the mightiest mountain in all of Balinor, it was the home of Naytin, the great dragon who guarded the most powerful talisman of all the Deep Magic, the Indigo Star. Not so long ago, the Shifter had stolen the Star, just as Naytin was waking from his thousand-year sleep to feed in Pearl Lake. The theft had upset the balance of magic and put all of Balinor in great danger. But brave Arianna had retrieved the Star and given it back to Naytin. The great dragon slept again, and Ari and Chase could take up a new quest. A quest that was the most important of the young Princess's life so far.

In the vision, Arianna slept at the foot of Blue Mountain, curled against Chase's great bronze sides. Atalanta bent over the waters of the Pool, her silvery forelock brushing the water like the touch of a butterfly's wing.

At the foot of Blue Mountain, Ari slept and dreamed of roses. She dreamed she walked in a lovely garden, on a path of amethyst stone, which twisted and turned through bushes laden with violet blossoms. A faint, crystalline chime drew her down the path.

In her dream, Ari saw a twilight glow at the end of the path. "Atalanta!" she cried. She ran forward eagerly.

The beautiful Dreamspeaker appeared at the end of the path. Her deep violet eyes looked at Ari with love. Her crystal horn and the jewel at its base glowed with soft light. Ari skidded to a halt in front of the magical being. "I have missed you so much!"

"Friends who meet after a long parting should embrace," the unicorn said.

"May I?" Ari asked shyly. She drew near the unicorn and put her arms around the warm satiny neck. Atalanta breathed softly into her hair, three light breaths. Ari knew that this was the way unicorns greet those they truly love.

"Sit at my feet, Your Royal Highness," Atalanta said. "And I will speak of what is to come."

Ari sat down, wondering. The flowerlike scent of the unicorn was all around her. "By returning the Star to the great dragon Naytin, you and the Sunchaser have restored the balance of magic in Balinor. And — this is very important, Arianna — you saved the dragon's life from the Dragonslayers."

Ari blushed. "We had a lot of help," she said. "Lincoln, of course. I couldn't have a more wonderful collie, Dreamspeaker. And Finn, that boy, you know, who came from Deridia to join our cause. And even Lori Carmichael."

"Ah, yes. Our friend from beyond the Gap."

"She wants to go home, Dreamspeaker. Is there a way to send her back, now that the balance of magic has been restored?"

Atalanta's expression turned solemn, and Ari didn't like the sudden look of concern in her eyes.

4

"We will be able to help Lori in time, Arianna. But there is a task to accomplish before you will have the magic to send her home." The Dreamspeaker's voice was gentle. "The war with the Shifter is far from over. Now he is more dangerous than ever."

Ari's heart sank. "How can this be? I've got the Royal Scepter. Why won't he give up now? If the Shifter tells me where my family is, if he frees them from imprisonment, I'm sure they will forgive him. There can be peace in the land."

"We all want peace," Atalanta said. Her silvery mane blew gently in the breeze. "All but the Shifter. He has spent a long time building his army of Shadow unicorns and his legion of evil human warriors. Now that he must fight without Deep Magic, he will fight even harder than before."

Ari sighed. There was a part of her — a very large part — that wanted to be an ordinary person — a person who didn't have to fight this seemingly endless evil. But she was the Princess, and this was her destiny. "What can we do to stop him?"

"You must join the trio of gold rings to the Royal Scepter. This is a rite of passage for all the Royal Princesses, Arianna. Your mother, the Queen, accomplished this when she was your age. It is part of learning to use the Deep Magic, on which your people depend. This joining must occur soon. But it will be under dangerous conditions, because of the Shifter. If his army can strike quickly and bring down the good people of Balinor, he can capture you and reclaim the Scepter. And without the Scepter, you are lost."

"The trio of gold rings — I've never heard of that before." Ari's memory had been destroyed on her first trip through the Gap, where she had been sent by Atalanta to keep her in safety from the Shifter. Her memory had still not completely returned, although she was beginning to recall things about her past, her childhood, things her mother and father — the King and Queen of Balinor — had told her, and the times she had spent with her brothers. Real memories! Ari was beginning to remember who she was — not just the lonely stable hand from the Glacier River Farm on the other side of the Gap, but Arianna, Royal Princess of Balinor. It frustrated her that the Scepter had not returned all of her memories as she had hoped, but until she had full use of the Deep Magic, she would not remember all.

Atalanta sighed. In Ari's dream, the unicorn's breath smelled of lavender. "The Shifter will strike swiftly. Time is your enemy. You must join the trio of gold rings to the Royal Scepter and use the magic against the Shifter, or his army will be too strong to defeat." The violet-silver glow surrounding Atalanta began to fade. Ari knew that this meant her time with the Dreamspeaker was ending.

"How do I find the rings?" Ari asked desperately.

"You don't, my child. The rings will find you.

They will come to you only when you earn them. It's part of the Deep Magic."

"There's nothing I can do?"

"You must start now, Arianna. Your first task is to travel to Balinor and help Samlett organize the Resistance. They must be prepared for the Shifter's attack or suffer a horrible defeat. Then you must search and find Dr. Bohnes. She will help you understand how to use the Scepter's magic. It is through the Scepter and the three rings that you will be able to find your family — your parents and brothers. If all goes well and the trio of gold rings finds you worthy, we may finally defeat the Shifter."

Ari had been feeling so good about herself. Now the trouble with the Shifter and his horrible army was starting all over again. Why wouldn't the Shifter just go away? Why couldn't Ari find her family and make everything all right again? She tried not to let her sadness show. "Atalanta, I miss my parents. I miss my brothers. Will the Deep Magic really help me find them?"

"Don't be sad, Arianna." Atalanta was a glimmer of light now. Ari felt the Dreamspeaker's breath stir her hair. "You've done so well. You should be proud of your accomplishments. But the battle for truth and justice, for good over evil, is an endless one. You must be relentless, just as your enemies are — even more so.

"Be swift and sure," Atalanta's voice was fading from Ari's dream like the chiming of a distant bell. "So far the battles of good and evil have been fought on a small stage. Soon the stage will grow much larger . . . the stakes will rise . . . you must not falter. . . ."

The silvery light faded entirely.

Atalanta was gone.

"I'll try," Ari said to the air where the Celestial unicorn had stood. And she meant it. She would always try. She had no choice.

Ari awoke with a jerk of her head. Chase stirred beside her. She rubbed his withers affectionately. Lincoln, her collie, was a warm bulk at her feet. Where was she? Oh, yes, on the outskirts of the Valley of Fear, on the other side of Blue Mountain. Soon she and her Bonded unicorn, the Sunchaser, would break camp and begin a long day's journey. Lori and Finn were also with her. They all hoped to meet Captain Tredwell and his ship, the *Dawnwalker*, where the sloping side of the mountain met the sea. Then it was on to Balinor Village, where much work lay ahead.

Ari picked up the Royal Scepter at her side and gently caressed the unicorn head. "Will I ever find my family?"

The unicorn's lapis lazuli eyes snapped open and stared at Ari. "What kind of a question is that? That's like asking me what direction we're traveling. If you travel long enough toward the east, sooner or later you'll be traveling west. Eventually everything comes around."

"I should have known not to ask that question," said Ari.

Suddenly, the sun crept over the horizon and it was time to get up. Lincoln rose, yawned, and stretched his forelegs. Twigs and burrs stuck to his black-and-mahogany coat. Ari pulled a few out with her fingers.

"I'm hungry," he said, wagging his tail. "Can you brush me later?"

"Sure, Linc."

He licked Ari's cheek and loped off to wake Finn and Lori. They were all exhausted after their encounter with Naytin the dragon, and they had slept hard.

Ari tucked the Scepter away and decided that she was hungry, too. This stretch of land near the mountain was filled with fresh berries and sweet roots. She and the others would search them out and have a fine breakfast. After they ate, they could all take a refreshing swim in Pearl Lake. For a while, she would pretend that the Shifter and his shadow forces were a distant memory. Just for a while. Then she and Chase would take up the fight once again.

2

"I'm so sick of this road I could scream!" Lori Carmichael bounced along next to Ari and Chase on the road back to Balinor Village. She was riding a unicorn rented from a stable-for-hire in Sixton. His name was Meadow, and he was an amiable sort, a Worker unicorn who had fallen on hard times when his old master died and had been forced to hire himself out for trips like this one.

Meadow had been very shy of taking a journey with Chase; although Chase and Ari both traveled incognito, it was hard to hide Chase's magnificence. He was the biggest unicorn in Balinor; his horn was ebony, and the jewel that held his personal magic was a dark majestic ruby. Ari kept the jewel concealed by rubbing dark oil over it every night, but there wasn't much she could do about his flowing bronze-colored mane and tail.

Meadow mumbled shyly when Chase spoke to him; Ari supposed the poor unicorn would fall over in a dead faint if he knew his traveling companion was Lord of the Animals.

"How long before we get there?"Lori whined. Her blond hair was tucked into a ponytail. She was wearing the blue dress the Innkeeper Samlett had given her back in Balinor, and she kept complaining that she couldn't ride properly in a dress. She and Ari were both trying to save their riding breeches from more wear; they'd been wearing the breeches when they'd first come to Balinor through the Gap, and the cloth was wearing out from all their adventures.

"How long?"she whined again.

"Very soon," Finn answered cheerfully. Ari had named the red-haired boy captain of the cavalry. He had done many great services for her and Chase in the recent past. He patted the great unicorn Rednal cheerfully. Like Chase, Rednal was traveling in disguise. No one but Ari and Chase knew that Rednal was a Celestial unicorn, sent by Atalanta to help them through their troubles. "Lori, you could ride Rednal for a bit, if you like. I'm sure he wouldn't mind."

Rednal snorted, and then he jumped in the air and bucked. Finn shouted with laughter and held on to his mane. "Hey, boy! What's up?"

"Must have been a black fly," Rednal said

smoothly. "I'm sure that Lori wouldn't want to hurt Meadow's feelings by changing unicorns in mid-stream, so to speak."

"That's what you think," Meadow grumbled. He rolled his dark brown eyes at Ari in appeal. Ari smiled and shook her head. Lori rode like a sack of potatoes. Ari sympathized with Meadow, but they had to get home, and it wouldn't do for them to go changing mounts.

"It's just another few miles, Lori," she said. "And then we'll be home."

But was it really home? The Royal Palace was home. And the countryside they were passing through was filled with her people. They were out in the sunshine today, tending to chores and still clean-ing the remains of the dragon storm created by Naytin. The dragon had flown over the land of Bali-nor in a fearsome rage after he discovered the In-digo Star had been stolen. Wherever Ari and Chase stopped for fruit or bread, they heard how happy everyone was that the dragon had gone back to sleep in Blue Mountain.

"And may it be for another thousand years!" a little old man had said when they stopped for ap-ples. "Three cheers for the Dragonslayers!"

"We had a lot to do with it, you know!" Lori snapped. But Ari had nudged her into silence; it wouldn't do to have anyone know that they had been part of the task. No one knew who was loyal to the Shifter these days.

"Look! There's the sign to the Inn!" Ari said. She looked at it affectionately. THE UNICORN INN, it read. FINE FOOD AND DRINK. SAMLETT.

Samlett himself ran to greet them when they arrived at the courtyard in front of the Inn, dusty and weary with travel. Old Samlett was so nervous he could barely speak.

"I say — Your Royal Highness! Such a victory! Naytin is asleep again! But we have . . . we have . . ."

"Visitors," his wife, Runetta, said, taking over the conversation with a sigh. She was as round as old Samlett, but her cheeks were rosy. Her smooth white hair shone with health.

Samlett twisted his big brown mustache. "We must — I say — we must prepare you right away for an audience with — with —"

His wife saved him again by saying, "Ari, come with me, I'll explain everything." Then Runetta dragged Ari away.

Ari watched over her shoulder as Chase and Meadow were led to the stable, while Lori, Finn, and Lincoln stood in the courtyard with poor Samlett, trying to calm him down and find out what all the fuss was about.

"What's going on?" asked Ari after Runetta dragged her upstairs to her room. Runetta closed the door behind her. She was out of breath and trying to talk, but it was the Royal Scepter that answered.

"Why don't you just look in front of you?" said the unicorn head.

Before Ari could get annoyed at the Scepter for butting in, she looked up and saw the dress. It wasn't just any dress; it was a gown — the gown of a Royal Princess! It was a long, layered white garment beaded with pearls, with a fine, almond-colored silk sash tied around the waist and a long velvet skirt that fanned out luxuriously on the floor. The neck was made of lavender lace. Ari stepped forward, her mouth open in awe. She reached up and carefully touched the sleeve. The fabric lay so light and perfect in her hand she could barely hold it.

"It's so — it's so —"

"Royal," Runetta answered. "It's the dress of the Royal Princess, *Princess* Arianna of Balinor, and it's time you put it on." Runetta folded her arms under her considerable bosom with a no-nonsense air.

Ari gently took Runetta's hand. "No, if I put on that dress, I'll never take it off." Ari meant it as a joke, but as soon as she said it, she knew that in a sense it was perfectly true. As soon as she wore the Royal gown, people would know she was the Princess. There would be no turning back. She would not be able to hide anymore, not from anyone or anything.

Runetta grasped Ari's shoulders and looked into her eyes. "Let me tell you what has happened. Rumors, rumors, and more rumors are spreading throughout Balinor — about the dragon Naytin returning to his lair with the Indigo Star, the Shifter losing the Royal Scepter, the Shadow army preparing for an attack — and talk of the Princess alive and well, fighting secretly with the Resistance to defeat the Shifter."

Ari pulled away from Runetta. She was suddenly very frightened. "Maybe it's not the right thing to do — telling people who I am. Maybe it's too soon."

Runetta smiled kindly. "I know you're scared, but the truth can't be denied any longer. The lords have come to the Unicorn Inn to receive you."

Now Ari was really scared. "The lords?" Ari had another flash of memory: the Lords of the Great Houses of Balinor. There were seven of them. She remembered their sprawling halls built with colorful stones, their courtyards alive with brilliant flowers and neatly trimmed bushes. Each of the Great Houses maintained an army of knights. "I remember," said Ari. "There were seven, but now we are down to three, isn't that right? The Shifter has defeated four of the Great Houses. Only three remain."

"Good, Princess, yes, that's perfect," Runetta said, excitement in her voice. "How much do you remember? They will question you. They'll want proof that you're the Royal Princess before they pledge their support."

"Before they offer their knights to join the Resistance and fight the war against the Shifter?"

"Yes, yes, exactly. We *need* them, milady. We need them desperately."

Ari tried to think. She sat down on the bed and concentrated. She remembered visiting the castles with her father, the King of Balinor, and she remembered what some of the unicorns looked like, but that was all. "Their names . . . I can't remember their names."

Runetta sat next to Ari on the bed and held her hands. "There is Lord Artos of Artos House. He's a short, fat man with a jolly face. Do you remember? He's so short —"

"Yes!" Ari jumped up from the bed. "He's so short that during council he refuses to sit down. He stands on the chair. And he's got a high, squeaky voice like a chicken!"

"Right, Ari. That's Lord Artos. Then there's Lord Puckenstew. He used to be a knight in your father's court."

"Puckenstew . . . Puckenstew . . ." Ari said, thinking hard. "Yes, yes, of course! He's big and muscular, strong as an ox. He never lost a joust or a tournament. My father made him a lord after twenty years of dedicated service to the throne. He's a hairy man — hair all over his arms and legs and face. He looks like a bear."

"Very good, Ari. That's Lord Puckenstew of Puckenstew House. You've got him. Do you remember the last of them: Lord Rexel?"

Ari walked a nervous circle around her

room, trying not to look at the gorgeous Royal gown she so desperately wanted to wear but was afraid to put on. "Rexel. Why can't I remember Lord Rexel?"

"He's tall and gaunt," Runetta said. "And, well, a bit mean. Maybe that's why you can't remember him. He doesn't treat his servants or his unicorns very well. Makes them sleep in run-down quarters. He drives his knights hard, never gives them a day off."

Ari nodded. "It's coming back to me. My father has had some trouble with Rexel in the past, isn't that right? He's refused to obey some of the King's edicts, and he's enforced a few rules of his own that the other Great Houses don't agree with."

Runetta sighed. "That's Rexel, all right. He's a stubborn old fool — forgive me, Your Highness — it's not my place to say it, but it's true. He even refuses to call his —"

"He refuses to call his castle a House!" Ari clapped her hands together in triumph. Now she remembered him clearly. He was so skinny he looked like a skeleton, and he was as tall and bent as an old willow tree. "Castle Rexel, he calls it, even though he knows it's against tradition. The Great Houses are called just that, and only the Royal Family lives in a castle!"

"Oh, Ari, that's right, that's it exactly." She ran over and hugged Ari, squeezing her so tightly that Ari lost her breath. Ari had to fight back a rush of tears, as she always did when she remembered events and people from her childhood, from before her days at the Glacier River Farm.

Runetta finally let her go, and Ari noticed that the good woman had to brush a few tears of her own off her cheek. "Now," said Runetta, clearing her voice and straightening her housedress. "Let's get you out of those old clothes and into something more suitable for the Princess. Don't be afraid of the lords. One look at you in that Royal gown and they will know that you are Princess Arianna. They will know for sure."

"I hope so," Ari said. "Because sometimes I'm not even too sure myself who I am."

Ari walked slowly down the curving stairs to the great hall of the Inn. It was the same hall where the members of the Resistance had gathered only a few weeks ago, and the Dragonslayers had made their grand entrance.

Now it was Ari making the grand entrance. The hall was large and square and plain, except for some filigree carved into the wooden beams over-head. The lords were sitting at the head table. Ari watched their jaws drop as she approached. She'd seen herself in the mirror only a few moments ago, before she left her room, and couldn't believe the way she looked. She looked like an entirely different person — royalty.

"You look radiant," Runetta had said breathlessly. "There is no doubt you are the Royal Princess of Balinor. Now go show them."

Lord Puckenstew, the strong bear of a man, rose halfway out of his seat and openly gaped at her. Lord Artos was standing on his chair, as Ari had expected, and his short legs seemed to weaken and buckle just a bit. Only Lord Rexel's expression remained unmoved. His upper lip curled slightly, and one eyebrow rose above the other as his eyes inspected Ari in a way that made her cold and inexplicably frightened.

Outside, hordes of people had gathered. Ari could see them clambering at the windows of the meeting hall to get a glimpse of her. She supposed it would be this way for a long time. The Royal Family was believed to be imprisoned. If the people knew Princess Arianna had somehow escaped, they would look to her for hope and guidance. They would want to see her and believe that the Shifter could be defeated.

This wasn't a bad thing at all — in fact, it was what Ari had hoped for. But Ari wasn't sure if she knew how to handle it. She could feel their desperation pressing in on her, pushing through the windows, walls, and the large oak doors of the meeting hall. She wished that Chase was with her now, but her Bonded unicorn wasn't allowed to be with her during her interview with the lords. At least she had the Royal Scepter. It was funny how the rosewood staff gave her comfort now — as it had ever since their encounter with the Shifter in his tower — when for so long she had been wary of it.

"It's the Princess," mumbled Lord Puckenstew, still staring at Ari in astonishment.

Lord Artos nodded slowly. "I didn't really believe it. Not until now, anyway. I thought for sure this would be some magic trick of the Shifter's. But looking at her, there can be no doubt."

"Don't be so quick to make up your minds," Lord Rexel commented. "She might look like the Royal Princess, but before I pledge my castle and knights to her, I want proof."

"What more proof can I offer you?" Ari said. "Other than who I am?"

"Plenty." Rexel stood up from his chair. His Royal unicorn stepped back to give him room. Rexel was an old man with a long gray-black beard, and he used a cane to lean on. "What is the name of your mother's father?"

Ari hesitated.

"What is the name of your father's Bonded unicorn?" Rexel went on.

Ari concentrated as hard as she could, but names were the hardest things for her to remember. Places, faces, things she had done and words people had spoken to her were much quicker to come back. Ari shook her head. "I'm not sure. My memory is still incomplete. As I'm sure you've heard, Atalanta, the Celestial unicorn, used her magic to send me to the other side of the Gap, to hide me from the Shifter. My memory was damaged on the trip, but it's coming back slowly and —"

"Yes, so we've heard." Rexel's voice was harsh. "This is what Samlett, the Innkeeper, has told us. Maybe you've fooled him, but the Lords of the Great Houses are not so easily duped."

Ari glanced at the other lords. They looked concerned. She had to convince them. "I remember my mother and father, the King and Queen of Balinor, taking me to the market, to council meetings, to the theater in Balinor Village, on long morning unicorn rides along the castle grounds. I remember my brothers playing with me and teaching me how to use a sword. I remember wearing my Royal gown — the gown that I'm wearing right now — and dancing a waltz with Lord Puckenstew at the corn festival in the Royal Palace. It's true that I don't remember everything, but I know who I am. I know it's my responsibility to lead my people against the Shifter, to free my family, and to win back the throne of Balinor for all of the good people in this world who deserve peace and happiness."

"I remember that dance," Lord Puckenstew said. "And she has the Royal Scepter. What more proof do you need, Rexel?"

"I see the Royal Scepter," Rexel said with an air of dismissal. "So what? Not too long ago, the Shifter had it. Perhaps this child is part of the Shifter's legion, working secretly for him."

Lord Puckenstew frowned. "The Shifter would never give the Royal Scepter to anyone, let alone a child."

Rexel leveled his gaze at Ari. "Or maybe standing before us here is the Shifter himself . . . in disguise."

"To what purpose?" Puckenstew said, frustrated. "You're just looking for trouble."

Rexel shrugged. "Is it looking for trouble to make sure the Shifter is not trying to fool us? Four of the Great Houses have already fallen. Do you wish the last three to fall as well? I'm not saying she's *not* the Princess, I'm just saying that there's a *possibility* she's not."

"Nonsense." Puckenstew dropped his large fist on the sturdy oak table in front of him. "It is our duty to pledge our support and our knights to —"

"Yes, yes," Rexel said. "To pledge our support and our knights to the army of the Royal Family in defense of Balinor, blah, blah, blah. We're all familiar with the Royal canons. But I am well within my rights to deny that support if I am not convinced this girl is Princess Arianna."

Ari was tired of being talked about as if she weren't standing in the room. "What would it take to convince you, Lord Rexel?" she said.

"Ah . . ." Rexel raised one long, gaunt finger. "Now we've come to the point. I think a certificate signed by Dr. Bohnes is in order. Dr. Bohnes has known Princess Arianna all her life. She was her nurse, and she's the only one who can verify the identity of the true Princess beyond a doubt."

Shock and disappointment ran through Ari. "But Dr. Bohnes is in Luckon. That's a week's journey away. We need to start gathering our forces immediately. The Shifter is preparing for an attack. He could strike at any time. We must be prepared."

"That's all you know," Rexel said in a nasty way. "She's not in Luckon at all. Her family hasn't seen her for weeks. She is believed to be somewhere near Demonview, perhaps in Angelcane, perhaps not."

"Then I'll find her there," Ari said steadily. In her heart, she was despairing. Had she passed right by her old nurse on her way back to Balinor Village? How could she have missed her?

Rexel remained unmoved. His face was as rigid as stone. "How very convenient that the doctor is missing, that we have to act right away, and that you only remember certain things. . . ."

"Yes, I remember certain things." Ari's frustration was beginning to get the best of her. "I remember how you always gave my father a great deal of trouble. Now it seems you'd like to give the same sort of trouble to me."

For the first time, something other than cold indifference flashed in the eyes of Lord Rexel. Ari had seen something similar in the Shifter's eyes when she had taken back the Indigo Star and the Shifter woke up and stared at her. Hatred. But Ari did not shrink away from it. She had learned quite a bit about hatred. It was a weakness.

"Lord Artos," Ari said. "You have not commented. Do you believe I am an imposter?"

Puckenstew and Rexel turned to look at the short man standing on his chair. He cleared his throat and scratched at his wispy beard. "It's hard to say. No, I guess I don't think you're an imposter. I mean I suppose you are the true Princess. You look so much like her. You walk and talk and act like her. I can see the Royal Family in your face and in your eyes. But the lack of memories . . . this concerns me . . . I don't know . . . the Shifter is a crafty one. If you had the certificate from Dr. Bohnes, well, there would be no doubt, no doubt at all."

"And, in the meantime, the Shifter will be moving against us," grumbled Lord Puckenstew.

But Ari was no longer angry. She saw a way out, a compromise. "Then let me make a proposal to the Lords of the Great Houses: I will find Dr. Bohnes. Meanwhile, you will agree to join forces with the Resistance, help them prepare their defenses and train for battle. You will work directly with my captain of the cavalry for the Resistance. He is a young man by the name of Finn, and he rides the unicorn Rednal. If Dr. Bohnes claims I'm a fraud, you may take your knights and go home, leaving the Resistance to stand against the Shifter without you. But if the doctor says that I *am* the Princess Arianna, you will fight for me, side by side with Finn and his troops and the rest of the Resistance."

Lord Artos nodded and said, "That sounds perfectly reasonable to me. I accept."

Lord Puckenstew smiled broadly. "I accept, also!"

Rexel frowned, and Ari thought she saw his hatred flare again. He had no choice but to agree. Two of the Great Houses had pledged their support, and that was a majority. If Rexel refused to follow, he would be breaking a Royal canon. Being troublesome and breaking minor rules was one thing, but ignoring the Royal canons was a serious offense. The other lords wouldn't stand for it, and they'd turn against Rexel. He might not be a friend to the Royal Family, but he wasn't ready to be an enemy. Not yet, anyway.

"Very well," said Rexel. "I see I have no choice in the matter. I accept."

Ari smiled and curtsied. She turned around and saw all the people crushed up against the windows of the meeting hall, struggling to get a look at her. Ari raised the Royal Scepter above her head and waved to them. She could hear them cheering as she walked back to her room at the Unicorn Inn.

3

Entia, the Shifter, stalked from one end of his tower to the other. He was in the shape of a Shadow unicorn now — big, strong, dark, and evil. His iron hooves made dull thuds on the stone floor. Smoke escaped his nostrils. His wings hung heavy at his flanks. The hate in his heart made him ugly on the outside as well as on the inside.

He no longer had the Indigo Star or the Royal Scepter to feed him the magic he needed to make him the most powerful being in the world. He only had enough of his own magic coursing through him now to allow him to shift and fly.

His dream of total conquest was now in jeopardy. All because of that miserable Princess and her unicorn meddling in his affairs! Curse Atalanta for saving Arianna when she should have been captured with the rest of the Royal Family. It would all be over if not for Arianna and the Sunchaser! The

Shifter would be ruling the world, all the others bowing humbly at his hooves.

The Shifter heard a sound outside his tower door — footsteps coming up the steps. They were not the footsteps of his servant, but slower, heavier footfalls that sent his spine suddenly tingling. *This is not good*, thought the Shifter. *No, this is very bad indeed.* Not one of his servants or slaves would dare to approach him without leave!

The door to the Shifter's tower opened, its hinges creaking. A soft whine sounded in the ancient wood.

A long, cloaked shadow spilled into the room.

The Shadow Rider! Entia bared his teeth at him. The Shadow Rider was an ally, a being who had appeared to him long ago and offered its evil help.

For a long time, neither the Shifter nor the Shadow Rider spoke. They simply peered at each other across the darkness.

"I'm trying to decide whether to give you one last chance to succeed," said the Shadow Rider.

The Shifter laughed. "The war isn't over — in fact, it hasn't even begun. I don't need Deep Magic to prove I am the greatest warrior to ever live." He glanced at the Rider slyly. "But, of course, you can help."

"I think not." The Shadow Rider stepped fully into the room. "This war is not about you. It's about power, conquest, and crushing the enemy — none of which you've been able to accomplish."

The Shifter, in spite of his anger and self-confidence, shivered at the Shadow Rider's icy voice. The Rider had helped the Shifter plot the fall of the Royal Family, and it had turned the Lady Kylie into the Snakewoman so the Shifter could use her as a spy. The Rider had helped the Shifter to grow strong and build a conquering army second to none. Was the Shadow Rider so strong that it did not need to fear the Shifter's power?

"In a week's time, maybe sooner, we can march on Balinor Village in full force. Before the new moon rises over their pathetic little land, they'll be ours, and there will be no more challenge to the throne of Balinor!"

The Shadow Rider laughed. It wasn't a pleasant laugh at all; it made the sound of nightmares and gargoyles. The Shifter's blood ran cold as he tried to hide the feelings he so despised in other beings: fright, self-doubt, and desperation.

The Shadow Rider stepped forward and grabbed the Shifter's horn. The Shifter bellowed in rage. No one ever grabbed the horn of a unicorn. It was an insult. Those who tried risked being kicked or stomped or slashed or impaled. A unicorn was too strong to be held by the horn, and the Shifter was stronger than any unicorn in all of Balinor. The Shifter would have killed the Shadow Rider in that moment if he could have.

But the Shadow Rider's grip was strong.

And the Shifter couldn't move.

He felt something that he'd never felt before in his entire life — pain. The pain shot straight through from the tip of his horn to its base, into his forehead, down the rippling muscles of his chest and into his legs.

The Shifter buckled and fell to his knees.

"One more chance," said the Shadow Rider. "Defeat the Resistance, capture the Princess, and retrieve the Royal Scepter. If you fail, you will feel ten times the pain you're feeling now. Do you understand?"

"Yes," the Shifter grunted. His horn was on fire.

"Good." The Shadow Rider let go of him and Entia slumped to the floor.

The Shadow Rider walked out of the tower and down the steps, leaving the Shifter alone. And furious.

4

"**W**hy did Dr. Bohnes leave Luckon?" Lincoln asked them. Ari stood outside at the stables with Samlett, Runetta, and Finn. The big collie was worried. His deep brown eyes looked up at Ari in concern.

"We aren't sure why," Runetta said. "Some say that she has business with Minge, the Jewelwright. He moved his shop to Angelcane not long ago."

"I remember Minge," Ari said. "He put the broken pieces of Chase's horn back together again."

"A good man, old Minge!" Samlett said. "Are you sure about this, Your Royal Highness? Must you leave now?"

"I'm sure. There are . . . other reasons I have to see Dr. Bohnes."

Ari sighed heavily. Chase was at her side,

groomed, well fed, and ready to ride. It was night. The moon was high and bright, and Ari could see the stars in the sky. The air was warm and there was a slight breeze.

Ari was leaving in the middle of the night because at sunrise there would be crowds of people gathered at the Unicorn Inn, still trying to get a glimpse of their Princess. Secrecy was important. She didn't want anyone to know she was gone.

"I can't believe I have to leave again," Ari said.

Runetta hugged her in her strong arms. "Be careful, child. I worry so much about you."

"Don't fret, Runetta," Samlett said kindly. "The Princess will be with the Sunchaser and Lincoln. She couldn't be safer."

"Are you sure I can't go with you?" asked Finn. "I don't like the idea of you traveling without an escort all the way back to Demonview."

Ari surprised herself by almost accepting. It would have been nice to have Finn along with her on the trip. She could have spent some time alone with him, really gotten to know him. But there were more important things to think about. "That's kind of you, Finn, but you are my captain of the cavalry, and I need you here to work with the knights and prepare our defenses." She had told Finn about the deal she'd struck with the Lords of the Great Houses, and Finn had been so excited his face had turned almost as red as his hair.

"Thank you, Your Royal Highness. I won't disappoint you."

But Ari *was* disappointed. She thought that maybe Finn would insist on traveling with her, or at least put up more of a fuss.

Ari checked her pack to make sure she had all of her supplies — a few camping necessities, dried fruits and vegetables, some extra clothes, and, of course, the Royal Scepter. It would be a day's journey to the *Dawnwalker*, another day onboard to Echo Canyon, and then a three-day trek across the Forest of Fellows to Angelcane.

"Well, I guess this is it," said Ari.

"Not yet it isn't."

Ari turned around. Lori came walking down the path toward the stables in her breeches and boots and riding sweater — the same outfit she'd been wearing when she had originally crossed the Gap with Ari. She was carrying a pack of her own, messily stuffed and bursting at the seams.

"Lori, what are you doing here?" Ari said.

"I know what you're up to, Ari, and you're not going to get away with it. You're trying to slip out of town without me."

"No, I was just —"

"No way. You're not going to leave me for two weeks at this lousy Inn while you're off riding around with all that magic." She pointed at the Royal Scepter. "That's our ticket home, and I'm not letting it out of my sight. We're sticking together — whether you like it or not."

"Lori," said Samlett. "This is not the time for you to be thinking of yourself."

"That's right," Runetta scolded. "Ari has important things to do."

"So do I," Lori shot back.

Lincoln shook himself and growled. "We're pressed for time. We have to move quickly. You'll only slow us down."

"I agree with Lincoln," Chase said. He normally didn't say much about Lori one way or the other. "We'll have to wait for another unicorn to be prepared for riding and —"

"Hey," Lori interrupted, "I don't care what you guys think. I never wanted to be in this crummy Balinor to begin with. I have a right to go where I want. Isn't that right, Ari?"

They all looked at Ari. She hated being put on the spot by Lori Carmichael. The girl was rude, insensitive, and selfish, but it was Ari's fault she was here. She glanced at Finn, who was about to say something that would undoubtedly convince Lori to stay behind.

"It's all right," Ari said quickly. "Lori can come with us. Finn, will you prepare a unicorn for Lori, please? Meadow hasn't returned to Sixton yet. Perhaps he won't mind coming along with us."

Finn looked surprised, but nodded and

dashed into the stable with Samlett to fetch a unicorn for Lori.

"That's more like it." Lori dropped her pack in the dirt and crossed her arms.

"I'll put together another package of food." Runetta sighed and walked off toward the Inn.

In a few minutes they were ready to travel. Meadow had flatly refused to go back with Lori. His back was still sore from the way she'd bounced on him all the way to the village. Lori would be riding Stalwart, a strong, squat Worker unicorn with a broad back and an easy stride. Everyone hugged, except for Lori, who was still pouting, and they began their journey toward the Port of Sixton, where they would meet Captain Tredwell and the *Dawnwalker*.

"I want a better room this time," Lori complained as soon as she reached the end of the gangplank and stepped onto the deck of the *Dawnwalker*. Captain Tredwell looked taken aback for a moment but recovered quickly. "Ah, our friend Lori Carmichael is joining the Royal Princess on her journey. How good to have you back on the *Dawnwalker*."

"Don't try and sweet-talk me, Captain Tredwell," huffed Lori. "I want a room where I don't feel every wave in the sea."

"Well, I'll see what I can do." Captain Tredwell ordered one of his deckhands to lead Lori away to the best cabin on the ship. "You know the one I'm talking about," the captain told him. "The one that's steady even in the roughest storms."

"Right-oh, Cap'n, sir." The shipmate winked and led Lori away.

As soon as the pair walked out of earshot, Captain Tredwell turned to Ari. "I won't even ask why you brought *her* along. This is a very important journey, from what I understand. Off to see Dr. Bohnes, is it? A coming-out party for the Royal Princess of Balinor, perhaps? Well, you can count on the *Dawnwalker*. We'll have you to Heartbreak Harbor by this time tomorrow. It should be a safe journey through Echo Canyon and the Forest of Fellows. That's friendly territory."

"Thank you so much, Captain Tredwell. You've been so helpful. I can't begin to tell you how much I appreciate it."

He smiled broadly. "All in service to the Royal Family."

Chase and Stalwart were led to their hold. Ari and Lincoln went to their cabin for a long nap. Ari was so tired, and the water was so calm and gentle, that she slept for hours without realizing they'd left behind the Port of Sixton and shoved off to sea. When she finally woke, Lincoln was sitting up, staring at her, his ears slightly perked and his tongue hanging out.

Ari stretched and rubbed her eyes. She was still groggy from her deep slumber. "Well, what is it? Why are you looking at me like that?"

"Oh, nothing, nothing at all."

"What's on your mind?" She tickled him under his chin.

Lincoln snorted. "I was just wondering what was on *your* mind, bringing that insufferable Lori Carmichael along with us on this trip."

"I did what I thought was best," Ari answered stiffly.

"Best for whom?"

"Oh, Linc, I don't know." Ari stood and walked out of the cabin. The sun was up, and the deck glistened from the reflection of the sea. Ari could feel a nip of salt in the air and a stiff wind.

Lincoln trotted out behind her. "Sorry. Forget I said anything."

"No, it's all right. I shouldn't have snapped at you. The truth is, I didn't want Lori staying behind with Finn."

Lincoln nudged Ari's leg with his muzzle. "I won't pretend to understand the way humans feel about one another or why they do the things they do."

Ari patted Lincoln on the head and thanked him. "If there's one important thing for you to remember about why humans do the things they do, it's that sometimes they don't make any sense at all. They just don't."

Chase joined Ari and Lincoln on deck, and together they passed the time, gently caressed by the warm sun and soft sea breeze, no more than a few words passing between them.

But Ari knew that the peace wouldn't last forever. A storm was brewing — the Shifter's storm of war. Atalanta had said Entia was gathering his troops. Time was against Ari. She hoped that she would be able to reach Dr. Bohnes and get all the way back to Balinor, to her people, before the Shifter launched his attack. If she couldn't do it, all might be lost — the throne, the Scepter, the peaceful lives of so many people — and her family, her parents and brothers, who were imprisoned somewhere and who depended on her. She couldn't fail. She just couldn't.

5

Heartbreak Harbor was a small port town populated mostly by sailors and traders. Seafarers would stay for a few days at the seaside hotels, conduct business, eat at the taverns, listen to street music, and move on to their next destination. Dried food for sailors was in demand in the street shops, so Ari traded some of Runetta's prepared meals for fresh fish that they could cook later at night when they struck camp in Echo Canyon. After bargaining for several plump fish, they quickly left town and headed for the canyon that would lead them into the Forest of Fellows.

Ari rode Chase bareback, tired of the leather saddle. The others jogged along with her — Linc, Lori, and Stalwart. She spoke to Chase in her mind and asked him about Heartbreak Harbor. She couldn't remember anything about it and didn't want the others to know.

That's probably because you've never been here before. You've never been this far outside of Balinor.

Why not, Chase?

I'm sure the King and Queen would have gotten around to it sooner or later. You're still a young girl, Princess Arianna. You haven't seen the world yet.

Why is it called Heartbreak Harbor?

Long ago, there was a young Prince of the Royal Family — a distant relative of yours as a matter of fact — a young man by the name of Artman. He planned to meet his beautiful fiancée here and bring her back to Balinor for their wedding. Her name was Lillia, from the House of Lafendal. She arrived a day early, met a ship's captain, fell instantly in love with the man, and sailed off to sea with the captain the very next morning. Since then, the place has been known as Heartbreak Harbor. I don't think anyone remembers what it was called before then.

On their unicorns, Ari and Lori entered Echo Canyon with Lincoln trotting beside them. The sun was high and the insects buzzed around their ears.

"We'd better take it slow," Lori said. "I don't want to fall off this unicorn and hurt myself. The canyon looks pretty steep."

"I'm sure the unicorns won't go too fast, Lori. They're very smart. You can trust their instincts."

"Easy for you to say. You've got a Celestial unicorn. What have I got? Just a ratty old Worker."

Ari glanced back at Stalwart. He grumbled

and shook his mane, but stopped short of tossing Lori on the ground.

The canyon actually wasn't very steep at all. It was wide and sparsely covered with rocks, pine trees, wild bushes, and gnarly weeds. Squirrels scampered and birds darted among the trees. Their travel was made easy by a path that led through the canyon directly to the Forest of Fellows. In spite of Lori's concerns, they moved swiftly through the canyon for most of the afternoon. Ari asked Chase how long it would take them to reach the forest. "At our present pace, we could camp at sundown, rise early, and reach the Forest of Fellows by late morning," he answered.

As the sun dipped below the lip of the canyon, Ari found a comfortable place not too far off the main road, tucked neatly in a circle of chestnut trees and sweet-smelling flowers. The night was so warm that they didn't bother to set up their tents. They would be comfortable sleeping under the stars.

Lincoln struck out and gathered some sticks, Ari cleared a small patch of land and built a nest of twigs, and Chase sparked the fire to life with a touch of his unicorn horn. They cooked the fish and ate silently as night settled in.

"It's funny, I never liked camping out," Lori said. "No bathrooms or mirrors. No television or CD players. No pizza places. But I don't know. We've camped out so much in this weird world of yours, I think I'm starting to get used to it."

It was the first thing Lori had said since they'd started out that wasn't a complete and total complaint. Ari stretched and got comfortable next to the fire. "I'm glad you're starting to like Balinor, Lori."

"I said I was getting used to it, not that I like it. Why do you think I came along with you? Sooner or later, I want to get back to the other side of the Gap, back to *my* world. You know how this is your home and everything, and you want to find your family and live happily ever after? Well, my home and my family are somewhere else, and I want to get back to them, too."

Ari looked up at the dark blue evening and suddenly felt sorry for all the bad things she'd thought about Lori during their journey. It was true that Lori was horrid, but she was stuck in a different world, separated from her family, worried she might not get back, and afraid that when she did get back her parents would be angry with her. That was a lot of pressure to handle. Ari understood how bad pressure could feel.

Ari hugged the Royal Scepter to her chest. "Don't worry, Lori. We'll get you home soon, and when we do, everything will be all right. I promise."

All of a sudden, Ari heard a horrible cry. It was the desperate sound of an animal grieving. Ari sat up straight.

"What was that?" said Lori.

Lincoln, who had been curled up next to the fire, jumped up and peered intently into the darkness. Chase shivered and stood at attention. The cry came again, only this time it was a moan and a cry and a sob all at once.

"Chase," Ari said. "What is it?"

Chase didn't answer. He stood perfectly still with his horn up and his nostrils flared. Ari had never seen him so rigid and tense before. *Chase*, she thought to him, *is something wrong? Talk to me. Please.*

Yes, milady, something is wrong. Something is terribly wrong. Then, without another word, he galloped off into the wilderness.

"Chase, wait! Come back! Wait!" Ari shot to her feet and clutched the Scepter. "Linc, follow Chase, don't let him out of your sight."

Lincoln raced after him.

Lori stood up, too. "Hey, what's going on? Where is everybody going?"

Ari didn't look back. She squinted at the dark trees and underbrush, trying to spot Chase and Lincoln. "Lori, stay here and mind the fire. I have to find Chase."

"No way!" Lori hollered. "I'm not staying here all by myself."

Ari didn't have time to argue. Another cry echoed across the canyon. Ari ran toward it, hoping Chase was following the cry, too. It wasn't completely dark yet, but the brush was so thick, Ari couldn't see very far ahead. She glanced back to make sure she still knew where the fire was. She didn't want to get turned around and lost in the canyon at night.

"Scepter, where's Chase? Where did he go?"

"He went toward the cry," answered the unicorn head.

Another long peal of mournful sobbing. But this one sounded as if it had come from the opposite direction. Ari was beginning to understand why they called this place Echo Canyon. The sounds bounced all over the rocks and trees. "Chase!" she shouted. "Where are you?"

Look for my horn, he answered in her mind.

Ari looked all around her. There, off in the distance, she saw the glow of Sunchaser's horn among the trees. She ran toward him, not sure whether she was more relieved that she knew where he was, or more angry that he'd run off without her. Lori crashed along behind her.

She finally reached the clearing where Chase was standing.

"Why did you run off like that?" Ari demanded.

Lincoln barked sharply to get her attention. "Here — here — look here!"

Ari glanced down and gasped.

Two beautiful unicorn babies were curled up in a tangled swath of leaves and brush. One was soft red, the color of new cherries on a tree. The other was the flaxen shade of fall leaves. The baby unicorns weren't much bigger than Lincoln, who stood beside them, his ears up and his head tilted. Unicorn babies were born much smaller than the horses on the other side of the Gap. Their horns were tiny stubs on their foreheads.

Ari knelt beside them and patted the red unicorn's head. "Chase, what's wrong? Why are they crying? Where is their mother?"

"Their mother is gone," Chase answered. "I don't know where she is, or why she hasn't answered their cries."

"Well, we can't just leave them here all alone. Let's take them back by the fire. Lori, give me a hand, will you?"

Ari helped the little red unicorn to its feet, and Lori guided the flaxen one. Their tiny legs trembled, but they were able to walk. Lincoln was a good herding dog. He circled the unicorns and kept them going in the right direction. They sobbed all the way back to the fire.

"I think they're hungry," said Lincoln.

Ari nodded. "Of course. I should have thought of that."

"They need milk," Chase said. "They are old enough to graze, and to live on grass, but they're too terrified to do it by themselves."

"Hey." Lori smacked her hands together. "Runetta gave me a whole package of dried milk.

44

She said to add some water and warm it over the fire —"

"Lori, that's a great idea," Ari said. "Empty one of our water flasks, then we'll use the flask as a milk bottle."

Ari sat down between the unicorns and drew them close to her, trying to comfort them, but they were so hungry the only thing that would calm them was the milk.

Lori didn't complain about having to do all the work: mixing the milk and water, stirring it in a pan over the fire, and pouring it back into the flask. It didn't take her too long, and Ari rewarded her with the job of feeding the baby unicorns. As soon as they caught scent of the milk, the babies stopped crying and went for the bottle.

Ari couldn't believe how cute they were. The red unicorn had eyes of garnet, and the flaxen one's eyes were bright amber. They had short little manes, puffy forelocks, and big ears. Lori shifted the flask back and forth between them, and the tiny unicorns attacked it happily and hungrily. Lori laughed at them and cuddled with the unicorns as they gulped down the milk. Ari was surprised at how well Lori handled them. She seemed to naturally open her heart to the babies, which was something Ari hadn't seen Lori do with anyone or anything.

Ari stepped back from the fire to talk to Chase. "Chase, why were those unicorns left alone? Do you have any idea?"

45

"I have an idea, but I can't be sure. Maybe we should ask the Royal Scepter."

"Good thinking." Ari held the Scepter out in front of her. "Scepter, where is the baby unicorns' mother?"

"Gone," the unicorn head answered.

"We know that. What happened to her? I mean, is she around?"

"If you're asking whether she's alive, yes, I believe she is."

"Where is she, then?"

The Scepter hesitated. The unicorn head closed its lapis lazuli eyes and seemed to concentrate for a moment. "She's in the Forest of Fellows."

Ari was relieved that the mother was apparently alive and well, but that didn't tell her what she really wanted to know. "Why did she abandon her babies?"

This time the unicorn head did not need to think about it. "She's a Wild One."

"A Wild One?" said Ari. "What's that?"

"I can answer that question," Chase said. "I'm surprised you don't remember, but the Wild Ones are another breed of unicorn. They are different from the Workers, the Royal unicorns, and the Celestial unicorns. They live in the wilderness and can't be tamed. They're wild and free and live only by their own rules and laws."

The Wild Ones. Ari concentrated hard but

couldn't remember anything about them. "They aren't talked about much, are they, Chase?"

"No, milady, they're not. The Wild Ones are considered a breed apart and left alone. A few of them live in the Forest of Fellows and care nothing about civilization."

Ari sighed. "Well, just because she's a Wild One doesn't explain why she abandoned her babies. That's just not right, Chase. We certainly can't leave them. We'll have to take them with us, won't we?"

"No, we don't have to," answered the Scepter. "If we do, they'll slow us down. We don't have time to spare for baby-sitting."

"And if we don't take them with us?"

The Scepter apparently didn't want to answer that question, but finally did. "Well, you know what will happen. They could survive by themselves if they would just eat grass, but they are too sad and lonesome and scared to do it."

Ari walked back to the fire with Chase and Lincoln at her heels. The baby unicorns had fed from the flask and were sleeping peacefully, tucked in beside Lori. Each was curled up on either side. Lori lay fast asleep, too, snoring softly.

Ari ran her hands through her hair, trying to think. "Do you think we can find their mother in the Forest of Fellows, and convince her to take them back?"

"It's a fool's errand," the Scepter answered.

Ari smiled. "No more foolish than half the other things we've done together. We can't leave behind two helpless baby unicorns to die of starvation."

Chase laid his muzzle on Ari's shoulder. "Thank you, milady. Wild Ones though they be, they are unicorns, and I cannot turn my back on them."

Ari scratched Chase's chin. "I know, my friend, and I wouldn't ask you to. In the morning, we'll all travel together into the Forest of Fellows. For the rest of the night, let's try to get some sleep."

6

In the Celestial Valley, Atalanta stood before the Watching Pool. The Dreamspeaker's beautiful violet-and-lavender coat was radiant in the light of the dawn. Her long tail, thick mane, and majestic unicorn horn glimmered with silvery fire. The grass was thick and green beneath her hooves. The Crystal Arch that connected the Celestial Valley to the worlds above and below had turned the sky brilliant with morning color.

Numinor stood behind Atalanta and urged her forward. Numinor was Atalanta's mate, the Golden One, King of the Celestial Valley herd and Lord of the Sun. Numinor's coat was the golden color of the sun, and the jewel at the base of his horn was a yellow diamond, the rarest of all jewels.

Atalanta stepped to the rim of the Watching Pool and placed her horn into the magic waters. "I,

Atalanta the Dreamspeaker, call forth the Royal Princess, Princess Arianna of Balinor."

The pool churned at the touch of Atalanta's horn. The water swirled into a magical vision.

"I see her —" Atalanta said. "Arianna! She is in Echo Canyon with Sunchaser, near the border of the Forest of Fellows."

Numinor stepped closer. "Is she on her way to find Dr. Bohnes, then?"

"Yes. And she has the Royal Scepter."

"Good, very good."

"I agree," Atalanta said. "I can feel the trio of gold rings beginning to gather. Arianna is drawing them to her, Numinor. She is growing stronger."

"Excellent! Now the other. You must look for him."

"Are you sure, Numinor? Must we?"

"We've talked about this before. We must watch the Shifter carefully from now on."

Atalanta circled the image in the Watching Pool with her crystal horn. "I call forth the Shifter."

The Pool churned again, and another vision appeared. This time it was the Shifter at Castle Entia. He was standing on a ridge overlooking the Fiery Field, watching his Shadow unicorns and warriors practice their military drills. There were hundreds of unicorns and hundreds of people.

"The Shifter is preparing for war," Atalanta said.

Numinor stepped beside Atalanta and peered into the Watching Pool. "He has grown strong — too strong. We cannot wait any longer. Soon he will march on Balinor. We must be prepared. We must train for battle right away."

"I fear you are right," said Atalanta. "As much as I hate the idea of fighting a war, of risking the lives of the Celestial unicorns, we cannot allow the Shifter to take Balinor without a fight. The Princess is running out of time."

The vision in the Watching Pool slowly disappeared. Numinor leaped away from the water's edge and called upon the other unicorns. "Fellow Celestial unicorns!" he bellowed. "It is time to gather."

The sun had risen fully over the Celestial Valley. All the bands of the unicorns gathered at Numinor's command. Every morning, a new rainbow formed in the sky, reaching up beyond the Crystal Arch into the clouds where the One Who Rules looked down upon all below. This morning the rainbow was as brilliant as ever.

"I greet the rainbow!" cried Numinor.

"We welcome the sun," the unicorns replied.

And then they all sang together:

"Red and yellow, orange and green,
Purple, silver, and blue,
The rainbow we make defends those we guard,
In Balinor's cities and fields."

Numinor stepped forward proudly. "Fellow unicorns, when will we cross the Crystal Arch to walk to the earth below?"

"When the dwellers of Balinor need us!" shouted the unicorns. "We guard life! We guard freedom! We guard peace!"

"It is time!" Numinor responded. "The Shifter's forces are strong. Soon he will march on Balinor. We must be prepared. Today we begin training for war!"

The Celestial unicorns shouted as one, *"We will fight! Together we will fight!"*

Only Atalanta did not cheer. She hung her head low and walked off toward the Crystal Arch.

7

Ari woke early in the morning to the sound of the baby unicorns' wails. They were hungry again. Lori volunteered to prepare more milk and feed them. Ari was shocked — but pleased — at this mothering side of selfish Lori Carmichael. She wondered how long it would last.

After breakfast, they broke camp and continued their march toward the Forest of Fellows. Lincoln was invaluable in herding the baby unicorns along in a straight line, and Lori didn't complain at all, being so busy watching over the babies. By late morning, Ari and her traveling party were nearing the end of the canyon.

"What should we name the unicorns?" Lori said. "They really need names, I think."

"They might already have names," said Stalwart. Ari was surprised at the sound of the Worker unicorn's voice, a deep and sonorous baritone.

Those were the first words he'd spoken during the entire trip.

"Well, just in case they don't have names, we should call them something. We should call them . . ." Lori thought about it for a short time, and finally said, "Albright and Jenny. Jenny will be the yellow-brown one because my aunt Jenny has hair exactly that same color. The red unicorn will be Albright because she reminds me of Mr. Albright, my fourth-grade teacher, who always wore red. I mean, the man wore something red every day of his life. It was a little weird. But he was a nice teacher. Smart and kind of cute, too. I liked him."

"Albright and Jenny," said Ari. "I think those are fine names."

Stalwart huffed as if he didn't approve, but said nothing more.

Stalwart doesn't think those are appropriate unicorn names, Chase said privately to Ari. *Unicorn names follow family lines and are important to their clans. The names Albright and Jenny don't mean anything.*

I know, Chase. But they mean something to Lori. For the time being, if it makes Lori happy, I don't see anything wrong with calling them Albright and Jenny. Besides, these babies were abandoned and —

And when we find their mother, she will have the right to name them properly, if she hasn't already.

Ari was surprised at the nip of anger in

Chase's mind. He must be very upset about the abandoned baby unicorns. Ari decided to change the subject and leave him alone with his thoughts. They had just entered the woodlands, so Ari said, "Chase, why do they call this place the Forest of Fellows?"

"The Forest of Fellows was named long ago by the One Who Rules, who decreed that all are welcome to live in peace within its borders. There are hundreds and hundreds of different animals and tribes who live side by side in the forest. It is truly a land of solitude and peace."

A shriek of rage suddenly broke the solitude and peace. An arrow snapped past Ari's head and thunked into a tree trunk. Ari yelped and Chase reared back. Lori shouted, "Hey, what gives!" Lincoln barked and growled and looked around for something or someone to bite. The baby unicorns darted for the trees, confused by the sudden noise and commotion.

Two, three, four more arrows shot through the woods in front of them. Then angry sounds of shouting — war cries!

"What's going on, Chase?" Ari quickly dismounted and pulled her Bonded unicorn behind a tree. She looked around for Lori to make sure she was okay, but Lori was nowhere in sight. She and Stalwart had probably gone chasing after Albright and Jenny. Lincoln was gone, too.

"So much for living in peace," Chase said. "Arrows and cries of war in the Forest of Fellows. I've never heard of such a thing."

Ari held the rosewood staff out in front of her. "Scepter, what's going on?"

"A fight," said the unicorn head.

"I *know* that. Who's fighting? Why are they fighting?"

The Scepter's round eyes blinked. "Well, if you just look over there, you'll see that it's the centaurs who are fighting. If you want to know why, just ask them."

Ari looked through the trees, and then she saw them for the first time — the centaurs! Their upper bodies, from the waist up, looked just like the bodies of humans: broad chests, two arms and hands, ten fingers, and perfectly human heads. But their lower bodies, from the waist down, were those of horses: long torsos and backs, four legs and four hooves. Centaurs. Yes, Ari remembered something about them. Her father — or maybe her brothers — had told her tales about the strange beasts that lived only in the Forest of Fellows, half-human and half-horse. But why were they fighting?

They charged one another, dozens of centaurs, brandishing clubs and spears. Their clubs knocked loudly together, and they thrust their spears at one another.

Ari couldn't bear to watch. The sight of war was horrible to her. But she also knew if she turned her back on the centaurs, they would keep fighting, and if they kept fighting, someone would get hurt — maybe even Lori, Lincoln, Stalwart, or the baby unicorns, who might be anywhere.

"Chase, I'm going to put a stop to this."

"No, wait, don't go out there!"

But Ari had already stepped out from behind the tree, into the clearing where the battle between the centaurs was raging.

She raised the Royal Scepter high over her head. "Stop! I am Princess Arianna, Royal Princess of Balinor, and I command you to stop fighting immediately!"

Ari's voice sounded far more powerful than she felt. It shot out like a cannonball and echoed through the forest. The centaurs stopped fighting more out of surprise than anything else.

Now that Ari had the centaurs' attention, she didn't know what to say. It wasn't as if she had a lot of time to prepare a speech. At least she had stopped them from bashing one another.

One of the centaurs trotted forward, an angry scowl on his face. "You have no right to halt our battle. The Princess of Balinor has no authority over this land. No one does. The Forest of Fellows belongs to the One Who Rules. Leave now before you get hurt."

"What is your name?" said Ari.

The centaur stabbed his spear into the ground. "My name is Tenshi. Be gone, girl, or we will not be responsible for what happens to you."

Chase stepped up behind Ari, his muscles taut, his head held high, his mighty ebony horn a lethal-looking spear. His muscles glowed bronze in the shadowy forest.

"Well," Tenshi said. "Is this the great Sunchaser, Lord of the Animals? Although we have never met, it is an honor to see you in our humble forest." There was sarcasm in Tenshi's voice.

Chase rumbled angrily, "*Your* humble forest, is it? There was a time when the Forest of Fellows belonged to the One Who Rules. Have times changed so much that you feel no shame in breaking the Commandment of Peace?"

"You may be Lord of the Animals," Tenshi said, "but that gives you no authority over the centaurs. We are human and animal both."

"I have authority over anyone who threatens the Royal Princess."

Ari wondered how she had lost control of the situation so quickly. "Wait! I am here to stop a fight, not start one. It does not matter who has authority over whom." Ari strode past Tenshi into the middle of the battlefield. "No, I do not rule this land. But I'm carrying the Royal Scepter. The Scepter is a magic talisman given long ago by the One Who Rules to the Royal Family of Balinor. The Scepter's power taps into the Deep Magic that was born at the beginning of time. This Scepter gives me the authority to settle your dispute."

Ari took a deep breath. Her memory really was coming back more and more. She didn't know how she remembered all the details about the Scepter, but she knew it was true and she could help the centaurs settle their disagreement.

"I will act as a mediator," Ari went on. "I ask the leaders of both war parties to step forward into the center of the battlefield right now."

Tenshi shook his fist at her. "You have no right —"

"Enough, Tenshi," said another centaur, slogging forward in the mud. "The Princess has the Royal Scepter from the One Who Rules. She has a right to call an end to this battle and mediate our dispute." He trotted up to Ari and said, "My name is Evanji. It is right to obey the law of the One Who Rules."

Tenshi picked up his spear and stepped over to Evanji. "The old ways are dying. This girl will not change that. If it's talk you want, fine, we will talk. But in the end it won't matter."

"Good," said Ari. "Evanji, Tenshi, it is an honor to meet you, and an honor to settle your dispute. Do you both agree to be bound by my decision?"

"I agree," said Evanji, "to hear what you have to say. No more."

Tenshi hesitated. "I agree, also," he said at last. "For now."

"All right, Tenshi, since you are so angry, why don't you speak first? Tell me why you want to fight against your own brothers."

"These centaurs are my brothers in blood, but not in spirit." Tenshi squeezed the shaft of his long spear. "Evanji and his kind believe in the old ways. They refuse to change even the slightest bit. But there are many centaurs who believe it is time to embrace a new way of life. What is wrong with trading with the merchants from Angelcane? What is wrong with eating their food or using their medicine to help our sick? The old laws say we cannot mingle with others, but the world is changing, and other beings have much to offer."

"What is wrong with it? I'll tell you," Evanji responded. "That is not the way our forefathers wanted us to live. Centaurs are not meant to consort with humans or even unicorns. We are different. We are special. No offense, Princess Arianna, but we are a proud nation. Those centaurs who want to embrace a new way of life are insulting our ancestors."

"We have moved away from the old, dead ways!" Tenshi shouted. "Those of us who believe in the new ways have moved over the hill to the far field. But we need the spring water." Tenshi motioned behind him. "And we have a right to it."

Ari looked over her shoulder and saw the spring for the first time. It was a deep, natural well of water, clear and pristine, as large around as the main hall at the Unicorn Inn. One beautiful stream ran out of it, leading deep into the forest.

"They're stealing the water!" shouted Evanji, pounding his fist into his hand.

"We're not stealing anything," Tenshi argued. "For us to survive in our new homes, we require a water supply. All we're trying to do is dig a channel to divert some of the water to our land. There is plenty of spring water for everyone. Evanji would know this if he listened to the man from Angelcane who dug such a channel from the River Onyu to supply water for the people in his village."

"I am not an idiot," Evanji responded. "I know there is enough water. But the old ways forbid us to divert the sacred spring water from its natural course. It is against our laws. Tenshi knows this, and he tries to divert the water anyway."

Ari could feel a headache coming on. She was beginning to wonder why she'd stepped forward. Tenshi's people needed the water. There was no way around that. But Evanji's people were preserving the old ways. That was important, too. She could not choose in favor of one without hurting or insulting the other.

Just then, Ari saw Lori, Stalwart, Lincoln, and the two baby unicorns coming toward her through the forest. Lori was leading the way, and Lincoln kept Albright and Jenny in line close behind. Ari was so relieved she almost wept. At least she didn't have to worry about her friends being lost in the woods.

"All right," said Ari. "I have heard both your arguments. I will meet with my counsel and then return with an answer. Until that time, you will wait without raising your weapons."

Tenshi and Evanji scowled at each other and returned to their war parties.

Ari ran up to Lori and hugged her tight.

"Gee whiz," Lori said. "You don't have to squeeze me to death. I'm fine, and so are the babies."

"I was so worried," said Ari. "I thought you might get caught in the battle and get seriously hurt or —"

"Hey, forget it," Lori remarked casually. "Looks like the fight's over, anyway."

"For the moment." Ari leaned over and scratched Linc playfully behind the ears. "Good job, boy."

"Don't try to sweet-talk me," Lincoln said. "These little unicorns are a pain in the —"

"I'm sure we'll find their mother soon," Ari interrupted. "Now, come on, everyone, we have a problem to solve."

8

The Shifter flew out of his tower and landed on the Fiery Field. He looked out over his desert landscape and was pleased. He was still powerful. Although he no longer held the Royal Scepter or the Indigo Star, he still had his own shifting magic.

The Shifter strode to the edge of the Pit, his dark wings stretching and retracting in the smoky heat. He marched down into the Pit and past the Shadow unicorns that stood guard over the human and animal slaves. The slaves labored day and night shoveling coal to fuel the Shifter's blacksmiths and weapon makers and the furnaces that fed the Fiery Field.

It was not all magic that made Castle Entia strong. It took hard work and slave labor.

The Pit smelled like brimstone and animal sweat. The slaves worked sullenly in the dense heat. The Shifter ignored them. He was looking for one slave in particular, and he knew exactly where to find her.

The Lady Kylie was digging coal near a boulder in the middle of the Pit. Her gown was torn to shreds, and she was covered in soot. Lady Kylie, who was once the best friend of the Queen of Balinor, had turned into an evil villain coerced by the evil Shifter. And now she was his prisoner. A long iron chain looped around her waist. The chain was enchanted, born of the Shifter's own magic; it locked her into human form and prevented Kylie from transforming into the Snakewoman. Her black eyes were angry and afraid.

The Shifter knew how much she feared him.

He used his magic to shift his hoof into a human hand. Then he reached down and grabbed Kylie's hair, yanking her head so that she had no choice but to look at him.

"You failed," the Shifter snarled. "I sent you out to steal the Royal Scepter, and you came back empty-handed. I told you that if you failed, you would suffer."

"It was not my fault!" she hissed. "You told me to wait for the battle between the Dragonslayers and the great dragon Naytin — but the battle was never fought. Arianna came with the Indigo Star and stopped the battle before it could begin!"

"This is your excuse?" the Shifter asked. "You never thought to find another way to steal the Scepter? You decided instead to do nothing?"

Kylie winced in pain as the Shifter pulled her hair again. "Ack! If I could have stolen the Scepter I would have! Yes! I would have stolen it. But without the battle to distract everyone, I couldn't get close enough to steal the Scepter."

"So this is better? Rotting in the Pit? You are a fool!" The Shifter's voice shook the cavern. The floor tremored. Stones and dirt fell from the walls of the Pit. The slaves and the Shadow unicorns looked up at him with uncertainty.

Control, the Shifter told himself. He must not let anyone think he was desperate. No, that would not do. Desperation was the mark of weakness and doubt. Desperation was the first step toward defeat. Control.

"You are mistaken if you don't give me another chance," Kylie said coldly.

The Shifter let her go. "I will give you one more chance to steal the Royal Scepter. Your little stay here in the Pit will seem like nothing compared to what I will subject you to if you don't bring the Scepter back to me." The Shifter's voice was calm now, perhaps even more frightening than before because of it. "Do we have an understanding, Lady Kylie?"

"Yes, I understand perfectly."

"Good. Listen carefully. Soon I will march in full force against the Resistance. My warriors and Shadow unicorns shall attack the heart of their stronghold, Balinor Village. You must steal the

Scepter before the battle is engaged. Without the Royal Scepter to help them, there is no way they can stop me from destroying their forces."

"I will do it! I promise! You will reward me when it's done, will you not?" Her black eyes glittered with malice. "I will rule beside you in Castle Entia once again? Yes?"

"We shall see. What I want, Lady Kylie, is the Royal Scepter in my grasp. Or else . . ."

The Shifter pushed her away. She fell sprawling onto the floor of the Pit. Using his magic, he altered his hand into the shape of a huge, clawed fist, with horrible talons gleaming like hot iron spikes. He raised the claw high up over his head, then slashed down and severed the magical chain that held Kylie captive. "You are free to go," the Shifter said, "I will not be so kind if you fail again."

Then he stretched out his mighty wings and took flight.

9

"I don't see any way out of this," Ari said. She had gathered all of her friends together in the Forest of Fellows, and they sat in a circle while she explained the centaurs' dispute: Tenshi wanted to divert the spring water to his village, and Evanji said that diverting the water would violate the traditional ways of the centaurs.

Chase narrowed his eyes into a grave expression but had no suggestions on how to solve the problem. Lori had barely listened. The baby unicorns had curled up next to her, and she stroked their manes while they slept. Lincoln and Stalwart appeared frustrated and eager to get moving again. "Just tell them anything so we can travel," Stalwart said. "We have got an important job to do."

"Scepter," said Ari. "What should I do?"

The round blue eyes of the unicorn head glared at her. "Settle their dispute, as you promised."

"Can't you tell me how?"

"Sure. But I won't. Solving complex problems is what the Royal Princess does, not the Royal Scepter."

Ari sat cross-legged. She scratched at the dirt in front of her. How long would the centaurs wait for her to make up her mind? Her mind raced with possibilities.

Suddenly, Ari stood up and called Tenshi and Evanji to the middle of the battlefield. They stood face-to-face, almost snarling, as if at any moment they might pummel each other.

"I've made my decision," Ari stated. "This forest belongs to the One Who Rules. No one owns the spring water. You, Evanji, have no right to prevent Tenshi from sharing it."

"Ha!" spat Tenshi. "So Evanji must allow us to divert the spring."

Ari held up her hand. "Not exactly. If no one owns the water, that includes you, which means you have no right to divert it from its natural course."

Tenshi looked ready to explode. "Then we're right back where we started. If we must fight to use the water, we will fight!"

"So will we." Evanji snatched up his spear.

"Wait, hear me out," Ari said. "There is a way."

Tenshi stamped his hoof. "Let's hear it, then. We're wasting time."

Ari positioned the Royal Scepter out in front

of her. The centaurs looked ready to rip one another apart with their bare hands.

"This is my ruling," she said. "Evanji, if you do not wish Tenshi to divert the spring water, you will supply him with five of your centaurs every day for one year. These centaurs will fill large barrels with spring water and transport them over the hill to the far field — as much spring water as Tenshi's village needs, no more, no less."

"What? You expect my centaurs to act as servants to Tenshi's village?"

"No, it's a trade. In return for your five centaurs, Tenshi will send five of his centaurs to live in your village for one year. These five centaurs will study the old ways and make sure that when Tenshi makes a decision, he is aware of the traditional customs of the centaurs. In this way, both of you will be satisfied. The water can be shared without diverting the spring. Tenshi will have access to the water he needs without breaking the traditions of the ancient centaurs. And Evanji will be able to keep the old ways alive even with the centaurs who embrace a new way of life."

Ari took a deep breath. She had talked so fast — did any of it make sense, or was it all just blabbering? It seemed so reasonable to her. Ari glanced at Chase. There was a glint of pride in his eye.

Tenshi and Evanji stood motionless for a moment. They seemed thoughtful and maybe even a bit surprised.

"What happens at the end of one year?" Tenshi and Evanji said at almost the same time.

"At the end of one year you will meet again," Ari explained. "Right here in this field — *without* weapons. At that time, if you cannot come to a final agreement about the spring water, you will continue with the same arrangement for another year — five of Evanji's centaurs carrying the water, five of Tenshi's centaurs studying the old ways. After another year, you'll meet again. You will continue meeting every year, and the arrangement will continue, until both parties can agree on what to do with the spring water."

Evanji cleared his throat and said, "I will speak to my centaurs."

"As will I," said Tenshi.

Both centaurs walked back to their war parties and explained Princess Arianna's decision. It seemed to take them forever to return to the center of the battlefield. When they did return, their faces gave no clue as to what they thought about Ari's ruling. They crossed their arms in front of their chests, mirror images of each other.

"WE AGREE!" they both exclaimed in unison.

Ari felt a rush of joy and relief. She had done it! She had stopped the centaurs from battling! "Thank you," she said. "Thank you both for trusting me."

"It is a good solution,"Tenshi said. "You have honored your Royal Family."

"And you have honored the One Who Rules," Evanji added. "To show our gratitude, we would like to present you with a gift."

Ari hesitated. She didn't want or need a gift. The fact that she had stopped the war was gift enough. But at the last moment she remembered something her mother, the Queen of Balinor, had once told her: "Never turn down a gift presented to you in honor of the Royal Family. It is an insult to the gift-giver."

"Thank you," Ari said. "I appreciate your thoughtfulness."

Evanji reached into the leather satchel he carried at his side. When he pulled out his hand, he was holding an exquisite gold ring, shiny and thick and brilliant, as large around as the palm of Ari's hand. The sight of it took her breath away.

"It's . . . it's . . . *gorgeous,*" said Ari.

"Wow." Lori was finally taking an interest in what was going on. "That's gotta be worth a fortune."

It took Ari a moment to regain her composure. "This is such a wonderful gift. I don't know what to say. No, I mean yes — I *do* know what to say. On behalf of the Royal Family, I thank you for your kindness and I accept your generosity." This was what her mother used to say. Ari remembered the words exactly.

Chase came up beside Ari and breathed into

71

her hair. "You have done well, milady. Your parents would be proud of you. I am proud of you."

All of a sudden Ari wanted to cry. Chase was right. Her parents would have been proud of her if they were here, if they could have seen how she'd handled the centaurs. But they were still imprisoned somewhere by the Shifter. Ari desperately wanted to see her mother and father and brothers again, but there were so many things she had to do first: Find Dr. Bohnes. Return to Balinor and help organize the Resistance. Fight a war against the Shifter and his evil forces. Only then could she even begin looking for them. Her family seemed so far away. It wasn't right. It wasn't fair.

"Milady, are you all right?" said Chase.

"Yes, yes, of course," Ari answered. She took the gold ring from Evanji. "Thank you so much."

"If we can ever be of service to you," Tenshi said, "please let us know."

"There is one thing you might be able to help me with."

"Name it," said Evanji, stamping his hoof on the ground for emphasis. "We are at your service."

"Nothing more than a bit of information." Ari brushed her bronze-colored hair back behind her ears. "These baby unicorns. We found them abandoned in Echo Canyon. Do you know of a unicorn mother here in the Forest of Fellows, one of the Wild Ones, who might be missing her children?"

Evanji and Tenshi said they were sorry, but

didn't know of any such unicorn in the Forest of Fellows.

Then another centaur, one of Tenshi's soldiers, stepped forward and said, "I might know something about this unicorn."

"Step forward and speak," said Tenshi.

"My name is Foygi. I am a sentinel in Tenshi's army. Last night while patrolling on lookout, I heard the cry of a unicorn. It was a terrible shriek, a cry of anguish. I thought the unicorn might be hurt or in trouble, so I tried to follow the sound of its voice. But the cry stopped before I could find it. I do not know if this is the unicorn you seek, but it is possible the beast was not injured or in trouble at all. It is possible the unicorn was a mother, longing for her children."

"What direction did the cry come from?" Ari said.

"Follow the central trail north from here. That is the general direction. No more than five miles, I would guess. After that, I'm not sure."

Ari thanked the centaur for his information. Then she said farewell to Evanji and Tenshi, the two centaurs who, only moments ago, probably wanted to strike Ari as much as they wanted to destroy each other. Evanji and Tenshi bowed to her, and then the centaurs ran off in a flurry of hooves and dirt and mud, leaving Ari and her traveling companions alone in the clearing.

"Wow." Lincoln grinned. "That was quite a

welcome into the Forest of Fellows, the land of solitude and peace."

This was enough to get everyone laughing. Albright and Jenny woke up suddenly at the sound of loud voices and began to laugh, too. It had been a trying and stressful effort, dealing with the centaurs, and everyone seemed relieved it was over.

"Excuse me," said the Scepter, "aren't you all forgetting something? Am I the only one who is paying attention around here?"

Ari wasn't thrilled about the Royal Scepter being able to talk whenever it felt like it. Things were better when the Scepter had only been able to answer questions spoken directly to it, before the magic of the Indigo Star had given it the power to speak freely. Now the Scepter could say whatever it wanted, whenever it wanted, and the little unicorn head could be twice as annoying as it was before.

"What are we forgetting?" Ari asked. "Just tell us."

"The gold ring! Wake up! The gold ring!"

Ari looked down at the fabulous gold ring she was holding in her hand. Suddenly, Ari remembered the words Atalanta had spoken to her in her dream:

"If all goes well and the trio of gold rings finds you worthy, we may finally defeat the Shifter."

She looked from the gold ring to the Scepter and back again.

"Slip it over my head," the Scepter told her.

Ari slid the gold ring down the shaft of the Royal Scepter. The ring fit snugly into a circle that was cut into the rosewood. "The trio of gold rings," Ari said. "This is the first one."

"Exactly," the Scepter responded. "If you join the three rings to me, you will know the Deep Magic."

"So what?" Lori griped. "It's not doing us any good if we sit around here for the rest of our lives." She stood up and brushed the dirt and pine needles off her riding outfit. Albright and Jenny stood up with her and started whinnying. Their little voices were high and sweet. "Hungry, are we?" Lori said in a very loving way. "It's not lunchtime yet, but I can give you some milk to hold you over."

"Don't take too long," Chase said. "We're already far behind schedule. And we still have a unicorn mother to find."

Ari stared at the Royal Scepter with the brilliant gold ring around its shaft. She needed two more to complete the trio of gold rings. Atalanta had told her that the rings would find her — that she would earn them. Ari was beginning to understand. She had certainly earned the first one.

10

Ari thought a lot about Dr. Bohnes as they followed the central trail north through the Forest of Fellows. It had been a long time since Ari had seen her old friend. The kind and feisty old woman had nursed her through her injuries on the other side of the Gap, and had helped raise her in Balinor. The closer she got to Angelcane, the more she missed Dr. Bohnes.

The centaurs had told them to follow the path to Angelcane. It was well marked. She and Lori rode the unicorns, since the way was easy and the forest was safe.

Albright suddenly darted off the trail in playful pursuit of a squirrel. Jenny followed quickly behind, and Lincoln took off after them, grumbling and barking until they fell back in line.

"How much longer do we have to put up with these baby unicorns?" Lincoln asked when they had settled down again. "It's not that I mind baby-sitting, Ari. But they do take a lot of time."

"They're just trying to have some fun," Lori defended them. "You could be a little more understanding. You're very impatient for a dog."

Chase and Stalwart laughed, but Lincoln didn't find it very amusing. "All you're doing is feeding and petting them. I'm the one who has to chase them all over the forest."

Ari didn't want them to argue. The journey was difficult enough without petty squabbling. "I think we've come about five miles, haven't we?" she said to everyone.

"Five point one miles to be exact," the Scepter answered. "I was wondering when you were going to ask."

"You could have just said something," Ari answered.

"Yes," said the Scepter. "I could have, but I didn't."

Ari brought their march to a halt. "All right, I want everyone to be quiet and listen for a few minutes. Maybe we'll be able to hear the mother crying, as Foygi told us. I think we all need a break anyway. We've been traveling all afternoon."

They settled in a small clearing and got comfortable. Ari sat down and leaned her back against a large rock. Lori sat next to a pine tree with the baby unicorns right beside her. Lincoln hunkered down in the bramble, exhausted from the effort of keeping the babies in line. Chase and Stalwart stood to-gether and grazed on the wild grass. Soon the baby unicorns got up and went over to graze with the larger ones. Ari took this as a very good sign. They were feeling happy enough to eat grass.

Ari yawned. If they didn't move on soon, all she would want to do was sleep. Lincoln came over and licked her cheek.

"You were asleep," he said.

"Just resting my eyes," Ari replied.

"We should get going," said Lincoln. "We could travel at least another two or three hours before we lose daylight."

Chase walked over, his eyes serious. "I'm not sure that's such a good idea. If we don't find the mother to those two unicorns, we'll have to take them with us."

"We could leave them," Lincoln responded.

"What?" Lori got up and marched over. "If you don't want to watch them, that's one thing, but to just leave them stranded in the forest is — well, it's just plain mean."

"They're Wild Ones," said Lincoln reasonably. "They'll survive. They're already eating grass."

"But they've got no mother!" cried Lori.

Ari raised both hands to her head. "All right, all right, please, let's not argue. Give me a minute to think." To her surprise, everyone did, even loud-mouthed Lori.

Finally, Ari said, "Linc, you're right, we should

get moving. But two or three more hours aren't going to make much of a difference now, especially when we're all so tired. Foygi said that he heard the crying late at night. If we make camp here, there's a chance that we might hear the unicorn mother during the night. If we do, then we can try to return her children. But if we don't . . ." She rubbed her face. "We'll have to go forward without them in the morning."

"You mean leave them out here alone?" Stalwart said indignantly.

Ari nodded sadly. "I'm afraid so. We need to make better time than the babies will allow. They seem capable enough to survive and watch after each other. I don't like the idea of leaving such young ones in the forest where they might be lonesome and afraid, but we have no choice."

Stalwart huffed and puffed. "But . . . but . . . we can't just . . ."

Chase gave Stalwart a friendly nudge. "Come now, my friend. The Princess is right. I don't like the idea of leaving them behind, either, but we have a kingdom to think about. Soon there will be a struggle between good and evil. It's a struggle we can't afford to lose."

The muscles in Stalwart's broad neck and shoulders stiffened. "Seems to me that a kingdom worried about good and evil ought to start with its own little ones." Then he walked off, not intending to pursue the matter further.

Ari bit her lip. Albright gave a tiny whinny

and rolled luxuriously in the grass. Jenny seemed to be practicing jumping. She bounced happily around the clearing. "Am I wrong?" she muttered. "Am I wrong about this?"

"There are hard choices in life, milady. This is one of them."

"But is it the right one?"

"I believe so. These babies are Wild Ones. They'll get over their loneliness and fend for themselves. It's not an ideal solution. It's not a kind solution. But there is a kingdom at stake."

"Thank you, Chase." Ari stood up and shook the weariness out of her bones and muscles. She hugged Chase around the neck.

"All right, everyone," she said. "Let's set up camp. Lori, you and I will strike the tents, Linc, you gather sticks for the fire, and Stalwart, you watch the babies."

Soon they would be in Angelcane. Ari would see Dr. Bohnes again. Dr. Bohnes would sign a document of proof that she was the Princess of Balinor, and they would all return to the Unicorn Inn triumphant. Thinking about the good things was a lot easier than lingering over the bad.

11

A ri didn't know what time it was when she heard the cry. All she knew was that she was sound asleep — a dreamless sleep, so deep and impenetrable that she did not wake up on her own. Chase was nudging her with his horn, and Lincoln was barking in her ear. She stumbled to her feet to see Lori staring at her. The cry was truly dreadful. It was a cry of anguish and despair. The baby unicorns, Albright and Jenny, paced nervously around the camp. They seemed upset and confused.

Ari went over and gentled them with her hands. They looked up at her, their eyes pleading. "Chase, do you know what the babies are thinking? Can you read their minds?"

"Not in the same way that we can hear each other's thoughts, but I sense their turmoil. It's their mother. They recognize her cry. But they think that we're their family now, and they're not sure whether they should go to her."

"But they have to go!" Lori said urgently, surprising Ari. She thought that Lori might be selfish about keeping the babies to herself. But she wasn't. She ran over to Albright and Jenny, clapped her hands, and shouted, "Go! Go to your mother! What are you waiting for?"

The babies looked doubtful and bewildered. Lori stamped her feet and shouted, "Go! Go! Go! I said. Get out! Go to your mother!" She waved her arms frantically.

Suddenly, the baby unicorns sprang into the woods.

"They're going!" Stalwart shouted. "Nicely done, Lori. Now we must follow them to make sure the mother takes them back."

Chase turned to Ari. "He's right. The Wild Ones are not like us. If for some reason she has turned against them, doesn't want them . . ."

"Let's go, then." Ari snatched up the Royal Scepter. "Everyone!"

They all dashed after Albright and Jenny. Ari followed Sunchaser's bronze coat and ebony horn. They ran up a foothill and down a shallow ridge. Trees and rocks appeared out of nowhere as Ari tried to maneuver through the woodland without hurting herself. The others struggled along, too, calling out to one another to stay close together.

The mother's lonely cry again drifted through

the night air. "*Eeeeeeerrraaaaaaaaaaaahhh,*" she wept. "*Eeeeeeerrraaaaaaaaaaaahhh —*"

They were getting closer to her. Ari lost sight of Albright and Jenny, but she could see Chase — the flick of his tail, a flash of hooves — not too far ahead. She was out of breath, panting. Her legs felt like wood, but she refused to quit.

Suddenly, Ari tripped and crashed through a wall of thornbushes. The sharp branches scratched her arms, legs, and face. She fell heavily, tumbling into a cold stream. The water broke her fall. She came up drenched and disoriented. She spat water out of her mouth and looked up.

In front of her stood the largest unicorn Ari had ever seen. The mare was at least four or five hands taller than Chase. Her coat was cinnamon-red. Her mane and tail looked like snarled nests, the color of burnt wood. Her horn was old and battered, chipped and dented, from years of no human kindness to care for it. Wrapped around the base of her horn was a dirty gold ring.

The mother's muscles were as taut as corded steel. Ears flat back, she curled her lips over her teeth. An angry whinny escaped her lips. She whirled and kicked out with her iron-hard hooves. Ari had never seen a unicorn so angry. She must have thought she was under attack.

Chase was quick as lightning and he easily dodged the Wild One's kick. Stalwart was not so lucky. He took a hard blow to the withers and grunted in pain. Ari knew she had to get the baby unicorns in front of the angry mare. At the sight of her children she might calm down.

"Lori — the babies — where are they?"

"They're right here!" Lori came crashing through the thicket. Albright and Jenny were right behind her. As soon as they cleared the brush the mare screamed again. "No!" cried the mother. "Take them away! Take them away!"

Ari couldn't believe what she was hearing. How could a mother say that to her own children? The baby unicorns didn't know what to do except cry. They opened their tiny muzzles and sobbed as if their hearts would break.

Chase nudged Stalwart aside and said, "Back, everyone, stay back."

The mother kicked out again at Chase, but with a slight movement of his head the kick went sailing past him. "Wild One, what is your name?" Chase asked sternly.

She kicked out again and missed, this time almost losing her balance.

"Stand and speak to me!" Chase demanded. "I am the Sunchaser! Lord of the Animals in Balinor. Kin to the red band of the Rainbow herd. Herdmate of the Dreamspeaker herself!"

The mare's eyes rolled, showing the whites. She pawed the ground and snorted. Sweat streamed down her flanks. She calmed herself with an effort.

She stood with her head down until her breathing slowed, then said proudly, "I am Orion, Queen of the Wild Ones of the Forest of Fellows! See here — my badge of majesty!" She held her horn up. The gold ring glinted in the twilight.

"How is it that the Queen of the Wild Ones turns away her babies to fend for themselves so young?" Chase's voice was low and powerful. He moved in closer. Dangerously close, Ari thought.

"Chase, be careful," she said.

"You know nothing of the ways of the Wild Ones," Orion said angrily. "How dare you question my decisions!"

"I know that the Wild Ones love their young fiercely. How is it that your way is different?"

Chase's words seemed to strike her to the heart. She turned to look at Albright and Jenny. They were still crying softly. "You cannot know how deeply I love my children. You cannot. But this — this is a matter of honor!"

"The babies need you." Ari stepped forward, still dripping wet. "Without your love and care and protection, they might die in the woods, all alone, wondering why their mother abandoned them. What matter of honor could be more important than that?"

"They are old enough to graze. They are newly weaned. Now take them away! I cannot look at them!" Queen Orion shivered in anguish. "Please, take them away." Her voice was less angry now. There was pain in her words, despair. The worst of her fury was past.

Ari stepped next to Chase. She wiped the water off her face. "My name is Princess Arianna of Balinor. I'm carrying the Royal Scepter with me. Sunchaser is my Bonded unicorn. Please, tell us what's wrong. We've come to help. Tell us why you abandoned the unicorns."

The queen faced Ari and Chase. Sweat lathered her coat, and her breath came hard, but the madness was gone from her eyes. "Their father . . . their father, King of the Wild Ones . . . Timberland was his name. He was once a good unicorn, a leader, respected among his followers. But something happened. I cannot even bear to say it. . . ."

Chase stepped a little closer, close enough to rub his nose against her long, powerful neck. "You must tell us."

Queen Orion looked at her babies again and trembled. "His heart was corrupted by the Shifter. He is an evil one now. He has become a Shadow unicorn and serves in the Shifter's army."

A Shadow unicorn. Ari couldn't help but gasp. Lincoln moved nervously around Albright and Jenny. Lori stood beside Stalwart, whether for his protection or her own, Ari couldn't tell.

"He has shamed me," Queen Orion went on. "He has shamed the Wild Ones. He has shamed himself. I am honor-bound to abandon his offspring."

The queen's last words faltered. Queen Orion loved her children very much. That was why she was crying out for them every night. But the Wild Ones were a hard breed, Ari could tell. Their ways were rough. The queen was proud. Ari would have to give her good reasons to take her children back, better reasons than for abandoning them.

"Queen Orion, I know of this kind of honor. I know that abandoning your children is not an easy thing to do. But, please, allow me to appeal to three other kinds of honor."

The queen hesitated.

"From one Royal Family to another," Ari added.

Queen Orion slowly nodded. "I will hear what the Princess of Balinor has to say."

"First, I appeal to your honor as a queen. These babies are heirs to the title of your ruling family. You owe it to your followers to raise them to lead the Wild Ones."

"Our ways are different," Queen Orion said sadly. "If they can survive on their own in the wild, then they deserve to lead. They can return and claim what is rightfully theirs when the time comes."

"Then," Ari said, "I appeal to your honor as a Wild One. Your mate has abandoned you to become a Shadow unicorn. You owe it to your followers to make up for his mistake. The Shifter and Timberland are evil. They *want* you to abandon your children. They *want* them to suffer. It is better to love your children fiercely than to give the forces of evil even a small victory."

Queen Orion thought about this for a moment. "These words make sense. But I owe my followers something else as well. I owe them honor and respect. It would be an indignity for them to see their queen raising the children of a Shadow unicorn. They might fear that I was leading them into evil. As I'm sure you know, a good leader cannot leave doubts in the minds of those who trust her."

Ari nodded, but she also sensed the queen's resolve weakening. Orion kept looking at her babies. She wanted to care for them. She wanted to be convinced to take them back. "Then my final appeal is to you as a mother. There is no bond as strong or as cherished as that of a mother to her children. It is the one bond that rises above all others. When your children need you, the world disappears. You answer their call. You give them your heart and soul because you brought them into this world, and there is no one else who can ever love them better."

"My babies . . ." the great queen said. She was trembling all over now. Her love was overpowering every muscle and bone in her body.

"We have all been hurt by the Shifter," Ari said. "He has imprisoned my family. I have not seen my mother in a long time. Even now, as we prepare to fight a war against the Shifter, I long for her. I think about her every day. When I'm in trouble, I think, *What would my mother want me to do?* I dream of the day we'll be able to speak to each other again." To her own surprise, Ari started to cry. She fought back the tears.

"You are a truly special daughter," said the queen.

"Yes," Ari said. "I am my mother's daughter, special to her, just as your children are special to you. If you want to fight the Shifter, Queen Orion, fight him first with love. It is the one thing he cannot defeat. Then, when the time comes, take up arms against him and make him pay for the pain he has caused you and your family."

Ari's words shocked her — the truth in them, and the spite. She hadn't really thought before about how much she wanted to get back at the Shifter. The Shifter's pure evil had made her vengeful. She would have to be careful of that. Ari could not allow it to control her.

"I sense truth and wisdom in your words," Queen Orion said. She looked longingly at her children. They cried out to her. The great queen stepped toward them, slowly at first. The babies suddenly realized that their mother was coming. They leaped forward on their spindly legs and whinnied in joy. The queen dropped her muzzle to them and nuzzled their little necks, both at once.

Chase nudged Ari's shoulder. Her hair and clothes were still wet from her fall in the creek. "I believe I will burst with pride, milady."

"And I'm proud of you, the way you stood in

front of Queen Orion, not allowing her anger to get the best of either of you. We're a good team." She wrapped her arm around Chase's neck and rested her cheek against his face.

I know how much you miss your mother, the Queen, Chase thought to her, using their most personal way of speaking. *We will search for your mother and the Royal Family together. When the day comes that you are reunited, I will be by your side.*

I know you will, Chase. Thank you.

After a short time, Ari told Queen Orion that they must leave. They were on their way to Angelcane, and then they would have to journey all the way back to Balinor to fight against the Shifter.

The great queen stood before Ari and the others. She really was huge, a giant among unicorns.

"Are all of the Wild Ones as large as you are?" Ari asked.

"We are primarily a Draft unicorn breed," Orion admitted. "And our size has always been great although we have Worker, and even some Royal blood mixed among us. But I am the largest among us now that Timberland is gone. I want you to know that when the time comes to fight, the Wild Ones will be there for you and the rest of the Royal Family. I pledge my unicorns in the battle against the Shifter."

"Thank you so much," said Ari. "I'm hoping

that it won't come to war. I am doing all I can to prevent it."

Lori scowled. "You're doing all you can to get us into mess after mess. I'll give you that."

Everyone laughed — except Lori. Even Queen Orion smiled, and she didn't know Lori at all but could probably guess from just a few words what a pain she could be.

"You have reunited me with my children," said the queen. "For that, I would like to present you with a gift."

Ari bowed her head. "On behalf of the Royal Family, I thank you for your kindness and I accept your generosity."

Queen Orion knelt before Ari and lowered her head. Then she said, "Around my horn is a gold ring. It is my badge of majesty. It has been in the ruling family for generations. I give you this ring in gratitude."

Ari reached down and pulled the gold ring from the base of the queen's unicorn horn. It was dented and dirty, like the horn itself, but Ari could tell it was a magnificent piece of jewelry just by the weight and thickness of it.

"Ring number two!" the Scepter announced. "Put it on me, where it belongs!"

Ari held the ring up, so all could see. Then she slid the ring over the top of the unicorn head. It slid perfectly into place above the first gold ring that the centaurs had given her.

"*The rings will find you,*" Atalanta had said in her dream. "*They will come to you only when you earn them.*"

Ari knew that she had earned this one, too.

Soon dawn broke over the Forest of Fellows. Ari and her traveling companions were on the trail again. Only one more day's journey to Angelcane. Just one more day, and Ari would feel the strong and kindly arms of Dr. Bohnes around her again. Just one more day.

12

Atalanta stood at the foot of the Crystal Arch. Each morning, the Rainbow herd gathered there to greet the sun. The Celestial unicorns would stand side by side, each unicorn a member of a color band of the rainbow. The huge oak gateway towered over the Dreamspeaker. Through those doors, the Celestial unicorns could travel down to the world below, into Balinor Village, where the humans lived. But another stairway led up to where the One Who Rules resided.

But it was the Old Mare whom Atalanta wanted to see, wanted to talk to. "Old one," she called, "come to me. *Please*, come to me."

Atalanta waited for a long time. Her violet coat looked splendid in the afternoon sun. Her silvery mane rippled gently in the warm breeze.

Behind her, in the Celestial Valley, Numinor drilled the Celestial unicorns for battle. Atalanta heard the heavy fall of their hooves pounding the earth. She heard their horns striking together, like the clarion sound of giant bells ringing in a lonely steeple.

Atalanta did not call for the Old Mare of the Mountain again. She knew the Old Mare had heard her. She would either come or she wouldn't. Atalanta waited. She would wait for as long as she had to.

A boulder at the base of the arch began to take the shape of a unicorn — its head first, then its neck, body, and legs. At last, the boulder transformed into the Old Mare. Her shaggy coat and aged eyes looked weary.

"You called on me, Atalanta?" said the Old Mare. Her voice was light and airy, not at all what one would have expected from so elderly a unicorn with such weary eyes, but the Old Mare was special in many ways.

"Old one, the Shifter is marshaling his evil forces to make war on Balinor. I saw this in the Watching Pool. Numinor is preparing our beloved Celestial unicorns for battle even now as we speak. There seems no way out of this terrible war."

"Perhaps there is not."

"But there must be *something* you can do. You are so wise. You know so much. I've done all that you have asked. I have been a strong and confident leader in the face of great sadness and a time of fear. The Celestial unicorns are ready to fight if

94

they must. But there must be something you can do to stop this madness, to stop the war."

The Old Mare lowered her head. There was great sadness in her eyes. Her unicorn horn was colorless, almost translucent with age. "Some things are beyond the will of all beings. Unfortunately, the force of evil is one of those things that cannot be controlled. It must be fought, always fought. Sometimes evil is easily defeated in the face of goodness, but other times, when the evil has been given a chance to grow, to prosper, to infect those around it . . . well, there is no alternative but to risk life and limb in order to conquer it."

"There is no hope, then?" asked Atalanta. "There will be war?"

The Old Mare brightened a bit. "I didn't say there was no hope. Princess Arianna carries with her a great gift of diplomacy and unimaginable power — power beyond her wildest imagination. If there was ever a wild card, it is your clever Princess of Balinor."

"Is she the key, then? Is she the key to peace?" Atalanta asked, hope flaming in her heart.

"Perhaps." The Old Mare began to disappear, turning slowly from the soft flesh of a unicorn back into a rock at the foot of the Crystal Arch. Her voice was a mere thread. Atalanta had to lean forward to hear her. "She is the key to peace; she is the key to war; she is the key to victory and defeat. The future of the world rests on the girl's shoulders. When the

time comes, she will lead us all where we must go."
And then the Old Mare was gone, her transformation into stone complete.

Atalanta stayed beneath the Crystal Arch for a long time, until the sun set over the Celestial Valley and her mate, Numinor, came for her. They walked silently together and grazed in the fields. The evening was beautiful, the air cool and crisp and scented with wildflowers. The sounds of fighting and practicing for battle were swallowed by the night.

And there was a temporary peace in the Celestial Valley.

13

~~~

Angelcane had been a small village for many years. It was the place where the Jewelwright Minge now lived along with a handful of merchants, craftsmen, and farmers. But the channel that the people of Angelcane had constructed from the River Onyu — the channel Tenshi the centaur had mentioned — had brought much more than water to the village. It had brought more people, new buildings, and prosperity. Nice houses lined the roads. There were large shops with fancy signs. A large Inn sat in the middle of town.

Ari could hardly believe her eyes as she and her traveling companions made their way through the new streets. It was a busy, bustling place.

"Milady," said Chase. "Look there."

Ari turned and saw the Jewelwright's shop. "Oh, it's the Jewelwright Minge's shop! Remember him, Chase?"

"Yes, I remember him well. He repaired my jewel and horn. The last time I saw him, he was surrounded by the peace and quiet of Luckon; now he's surrounded by houses and a mercantile."

"Maybe he can tell us where Dr. Bohnes is," Lincoln said, wagging his tail.

Lori scrubbed the dirt of the journey from her face with both hands. "Maybe we can go to that fancy Inn and get a decent meal and a bath and maybe even a manicure," she said sourly. "It's late in the afternoon. There will be plenty of time tomorrow to track down that historical-artifact doctor of yours."

Lori had lost a lot of her charm ever since she had to say good-bye to Albright and Jenny. Queen Orion hadn't named her children, and as a way of thanking Lori for taking such good care of them, she decided to keep the names Lori had given them. It was a nice gesture, and even Lori thought so. But now she was back to her old cranky self.

Ari said, "Okay, why don't you go on ahead to the Inn, Lori. We'll join you in a few minutes."

"That would be great, except I don't have any money. They don't take Visa here, remember?"

Ari perched the Royal Scepter against her shoulder, reached into her bag, and pulled out several coins. "Here. This should cover a room of your own and the stable fee for Stalwart."

Lori grabbed the coins out of Ari's hand. "Hey, I didn't know you had money. What gives?"

"Runetta gave me some money before we left. She knew we'd probably need it once we got to Angelcane."

"Nice of you to share," Lori said sarcastically. "Come on, Stalwart, let's go get comfy."

"Thank the stars," Lincoln growled after they were gone. "Couldn't you have left that girl on the other side of the Gap?"

"I wish I could have, Linc, but she refused to stay behind."

"You should have knocked her out," the Scepter commented.

"Well!" Ari smiled. "Shame on you, for not having more regal patience."

"I don't know," Chase commented. "I think the Scepter has a good point."

They all laughed as they walked to Jewelwright Minge's shop. Ari and Lincoln stepped inside, but because Chase was too big to fit through the door, he stayed outside on the sidewalk, drawing stares from the people in the village. Chase was a magnificent sight with his blazing bronze-colored coat, ebony horn, and the brilliant ruby at the base of his unicorn horn. Sometimes Ari was so unbelievably proud to be bonded to Chase.

The shop was small and cluttered. Well-used tools were strewn about, and there were rags and boxes everywhere. There was a workbench in the middle of the shop where Jewelwright Minge sat, an old man with rounded shoulders, long gray hair, and a pair of spectacles that made his eyes look as big as breadfruit. The shop smelled strongly of the lemony liquid Minge used for cleaning jewelry.

"Jewelwright Minge, my name is Arianna. I saw you some months ago about a unicorn horn and a jewel that you repaired. I don't know if you remember me, but —"

"Of course I remember you, milady. I may be old, but I'm not daft — ha! It's good to see you again, and your dog, too."

"And it's good to see you," said Ari.

"Tell me," Jewelwright Minge said as he laid a tool on his bench, "how's that wonderful unicorn of yours doing . . . what was his name?"

"Sunchaser," Ari said. "He's just fine. Finer than ever, in fact, thanks to you."

The Jewelwright fiddled with the mallet and the small tap he'd been working with. The piece of jewelry on his workbench was a lovely copper bracelet ornamented with small round stones that looked like pearls. He wiped his hands on a greasy rag. "To what do I owe the pleasure of your visit to my shop?"

"We're looking for Dr. Bohnes, actually. We've just arrived and we need to see her as soon as possible. Do you have any idea where she's staying?"

"Ah, Dr. Bohnes . . ." Minge glanced down at his workbench. An oddly grim expression crossed his face.

"You do remember her, don't you, Jewel-wright Minge?"

Minge began fussing with a small tool, turning it this way and that in his hand. "She's staying in a small cottage just outside of the village. One of the village boys is there to help her with her chores. To find her, you walk past the hotel and keep going until you come to Deer Lane Park, where all the picnic tables are. Can't miss it. Go straight through the park and turn left, follow the dirt path for half a mile or so, and you'll see the cottage, very pretty, made of fieldstone, ivy running up the porch, a well, and a flower bed in the front yard —"

"Thank you, Jewelwright Minge," Ari interrupted, afraid that if she didn't slow him down he might go on forever. "Are you sure you're all right? You seem bothered by something."

"You should find Dr. Bohnes at the cottage."

He went to work on his bracelet. Ari shrugged. The meeting was obviously over. "It was very nice seeing you again. Thanks for the information. I'll stop in and say good-bye before we leave town."

"You do that," said Minge, without glancing up from his bench. "Yes, you be sure to do that, won't you?"

When they walked outside Lincoln said, "That was a little weird."

"Something wrong?" Chase asked.

Ari said, "I don't know. Something seemed to be bothering Jewelwright Minge, I guess. But I have no idea what it could be."

Chase flicked his ears at a bumblebee that was buzzing around his head. "Did you find out where Dr. Bohnes is staying?"

"Yes, and I'd like to go see her right now rather than waiting for morning. Linc, why don't you go to the hotel and let Lori know that Chase and I have gone to find Bohnesy at the cottage. Stay with her and try to keep her out of trouble. We'll be back as soon as we can."

"What have I done to deserve such punishment?" Linc said.

"I'll make it up to you," Ari said, petting him gently on the head. "Go on, now."

14

Ari and Chase found the dirt road that Jewelwright Minge had said would lead to Dr. Bohnes. Ari kept close to Chase as they hurried toward the cottage. Something was wrong here. She could feel it.

She whistled to divert herself, but stopped when Chase rolled his dark eye at her. She discovered that the Royal Scepter worked rather nicely as a walking stick. When she leaned against it, she felt a spring in her step that hadn't been there before. A cool breeze made the walk pleasant, along with the smell of evergreen bushes and wildflowers. The setting sun painted all the colors warm and lush. Ari tried to relax, to enjoy the walk. But she couldn't.

Something was very wrong.

The cottage Jewelwright Minge had described in such detail was a charming stone lodge with a cozy porch and climbing ivy. Ari combed her fingers through Chase's mane and tried to make him a little more tidy. The journey to get here had been hard on all of them. Dr. Bohnes didn't tolerate dirty animals, nor dirty human beings very well, and Ari hadn't had a bath in three days. She sighed. It was hopeless. She was a mess and would have to remain that way for now. "Wait here, Chase. I'm going inside to see Bohnesy. I'll be out in a few minutes."

"The grass looks sweet. I think I'll graze a bit."

Ari walked up the steps of the porch and knocked on the front door. She had missed old Bohnesy so much she hadn't wanted to think about it, had put it out of her mind as best she could so that it wouldn't hurt. Dr. Bohnes was the one link Ari had to her past, to her family, and even to the other side of the Gap.

A young boy answered the door. He had dusty hair and skinny arms and legs. The boy was holding a mop in one hand that was twice his height and a dirty rag in the other. "Help ya, mum?" he said, in a strange kind of accent Ari had never heard before.

"Um, yes, I'm looking for Dr. Bohnes."

"Who's owskin' for 'er," he asked in a rude manner, Ari thought.

"If you mean who is asking for Dr. Bohnes, my name is Arianna. I'm one of Dr. Bohnes's best friends. I'm sure she'll want to see me so if I could just come in and —"

"Ow right then, wait here, mum, while I go check fer ya." Then he closed the door in Ari's face.

Ari pursed her lips and muttered to herself, "Can you believe that boy?"

"Sure," said the Scepter. "He's going to check if Dr. Bohnes wants to see you. Pretty straightforward. Very believable."

Ari shook her head. "Forget I asked."

The boy returned and opened the door again. "I guess it's owright to come in, mum."

Ari walked past him into the small cottage. It was beautiful inside, with handcrafted furniture, richly dark, everything incredibly neat and spotless. If the boy was responsible for the tidiness, Ari could forgive him his rudeness. But Ari was impatient to see her old friend now. "Where is she?"

"This way. Follow me."

The boy led Ari into a quaint sitting room where Dr. Bohnes was seated in a tall rocking chair. She smiled at Ari, her hair a little whiter, it seemed, than Ari remembered it. And it looked as if she had lost quite a bit of weight — she seemed gaunt, in fact. But it was so good to see her!

Ari ran over and wrapped her arms around Dr. Bohnes.

"Ari, sweetheart, it's so wonderful to see you again."

"I've missed you so much, Dr. Bohnes."

"Please do forgive Varto. He's a good boy, but maybe a bit overprotective of me."

"I can't fault him for that," Ari said. She noticed that Bohnesy hadn't hugged her in return. And

105

it was a pleasant evening but the doctor had a blanket wrapped around her. Dr. Bohnes coughed suddenly, a horrible chest cough that seemed to rattle her ribs.

"Bohnesy, aren't you feeling well?" said Ari.

Dr. Bohnes glanced up at the young boy. "You can leave us alone now, Varto."

"Can I get you some tea?" said the boy. "You and the miss?"

"That would be nice, thank you."

Ari sat in a small chair opposite Dr. Bohnes. *Something* was *wrong here,* she thought. She had been right to be anxious. Dr. Bohnes reached out and grasped Ari's hands. The doctor's skin felt cold and clammy.

"What is it, Bohnesy? What's wrong?"

"You can see that I'm sick," she said in her old blunt way. "I didn't want to tell you before because I knew you would worry about me. I knew it would distract you in this terrible time when you have so many other things to worry about."

"Bohnesy, no! You should have told me. I would have come right away!"

The doctor coughed again and this time her whole body shook. Her face reflected the pain, although she tried to hide it. "That's exactly why I didn't tell you. Balinor needs you now more than I do."

"That's ridiculous. Look at you. You're gaunt and pale as a ghost. And that cough is horrible.

Where's that boy? He's going to set up a room for me at once, and I'm going to nurse you back to health."

"Ari, you can't."

"Nonsense, I'm the Princess of Balinor." Ari stamped the butt of the Royal Scepter on the floor.

Dr. Bohnes managed a smile. "Look at that . . . you've found two gold rings for the Scepter! I knew you could do it."

"Well, I didn't really find them. They found me, kind of. That's the way Atalanta described it in my dream, anyway. And she was right, of course, just like always."

"This is wonderful, Ari. You really are becoming the Royal Princess."

"Yes, well, don't change the subject."

"Ari," Dr. Bohnes said, "you came all this way, now you must listen."

"But —"

"No buts. Hear me out."

Varto returned with their tea on a beautiful pewter tray. He set their cups on a small serving table. Bohnesy turned to the boy and said, "Varto, can you please bring me the small chest on my bureau?"

"Yes, mum." He scampered off again.

Ari felt awful and helpless. The sight of Dr. Bohnes sick was making *her* sick. "I don't understand. Why can't you use your magic to make you well?"

"I won't sugarcoat the truth, Ari. I have been

using my magic. In fact, it's taking all the magic I've got just to keep me sitting up in this chair."

"Well, I've got more magic. With the Royal Scepter I'm sure we can figure out what the problem is and fix you up."

"Ari, you must understand, there are some things that not even magic can fix."

"What are you saying?"

Varto came back into the sitting room. He was carrying a small wooden chest, ornamented with graceful lines of silver and gold. He placed the chest gently in the doctor's lap and retreated again.

Dr. Bohnes reached up and brushed her fingers through Ari's bronze-colored hair. "You're becoming such a beautiful young woman." She opened the chest. Inside the box a shiny gold ring sparkled. Ari could see right away that it was the same size as the two other gold rings on the Scepter.

"The third ring!" said the Royal Scepter. "Put it on me, where it belongs."

Ari looked from the gold ring to Dr. Bohnes. "You've got the third ring? Have you always had it?"

"Yes, my dear. But I couldn't give it to you until now."

"Why not?"

"Because this is the third test, and it's up to me to test you."

"What kind of a test?"

"It's simple," the Scepter decided to answer.

"When the trio of gold rings joins with the Royal Scepter, you will have the authority to rule over all of Balinor. You won't just be the Princess anymore."

"Is that true, Doctor?" Ari said.

"Yes, but you'll have to earn this ring, just like the others."

"How?"

Dr. Bohnes removed the ring from the box and held it out to her. "You have to put the ring on the Royal Scepter, and then you have to leave me here and return to Balinor to lead your people."

Ari shook her head. "No, no, I won't do it. I won't leave you behind. I can stay here and help you get better if —"

"Ari, take the ring."

The gold seemed to come to life in the doctor's hand. It shimmered and caused the other rings to glow in the dim light of the sitting room. Ari could hear birds twittering outside, and it suddenly looked like it might rain.

"But I can't leave you behind when you're sick." Ari couldn't stop the tears from filling her eyes.

Bohnesy's face reflected kindness and understanding, but firmness as well. Ari could see that the old woman was not about to back down. "The most difficult decisions you'll ever make lie ahead of you. If you can't make this one — for the good of Balinor, for the good of the world — you have no business ruling."

Ari wiped the tears from her eyes. "But who will train me how to use the Royal Scepter? I need to know how to use the Deep Magic to find my parents, my family. You have to teach me!"

Dr. Bohnes shook her head. "No one really needs to show you how to use the Scepter. It works in much the same way as the rings. The rings found you when you were ready to receive them, when you were worthy. The magic will find you, too, when you're ready. You must trust yourself and follow your instincts."

"No. You've helped me all my life. You nursed me through those horrible injuries on the other side of the Gap. You've always been there for me when I've needed you. Now you need me."

Dr. Bohnes shrugged. "It's up to you. You're old enough to make your own decisions. If you stay, events will transpire without you. The war between good and evil will go on. You'll sit here with a sick old woman and wait to see what happens. Or you'll take this ring and put it where it belongs, and go lead the fight against the Shifter. It's up to you."

The Royal Scepter began vibrating in Ari's hand, almost seething with the power of the trio of gold rings. Ari knew what she had to do. It was horrible — just horrible. How could she leave her dear friend behind when she was so awfully sick, when not even magic could help cure her? But what choice did Ari have? She couldn't turn her back on

Balinor. The Shifter might win the war if she did. Then everyone would suffer. Everyone, everywhere.

Ari stood up and paced to the window. The rain had begun to fall in thin sheets, pattering on the roof and the windows. She saw Chase outside, his handsome face raised up to the sky, enjoying the shower.

"I need a document with your seal, Bohnesy, that says you've examined me and I'm the real Princess of Balinor. Lord Rexel refuses to pledge his knights to the fight against the Shifter until he has your assurance that I'm not an imposter."

"Ah, good old Lord Rexel. Watch him carefully, Arianna. He likes power — a terrible weakness in the face of evil."

"I'll watch him closely. I've seen something in his eyes that I don't like."

Dr. Bohnes reached into her small chest again and removed a parchment. "Here's the document you'll need for the Lords of the Great Houses. I prepared it ahead of time."

"You knew they'd want proof?"

"I suspected."

Ari walked over and took the document.

"The ring!" the Scepter insisted. "Take the ring and put it on me, will you? What are you waiting for?"

Ari accepted the ring and felt the magic surge up her arm and through her entire body. She slipped the final gold band over the unicorn head, and it fit perfectly in place with the other rings. The Royal Scepter sparkled with new magic; its rosewood flared like a torch; the lapis lazuli eyes of the unicorn head turned fiercely brilliant with hot blue magic.

Ari was afraid to hold the staff in her hands. She almost dropped it on the floor. But in a moment, nothing more than the blink of an eye, the Royal Scepter became a part of her. It became more than just a symbol of her power and the emblem of the Royal Family. It became the truth of her existence and the measure of her strength. It became her life and breath. She knew it would forever change her relationship with the world, in ways she could not even begin to imagine.

"I am so very, very proud of you, Princess Arianna," said Dr. Bohnes. Her voice was stronger. A sparkle was back in her bright blue eyes.

"Do you need anything?" Ari asked.

"I'm already feeling better, now that you've passed the third test!" Ari wanted to weep with relief. Dr. Bohnes smiled. "Varto and I have done fine so far without you. I think it's best if you leave now, before we get too sentimental. Good-byes are difficult."

Ari knelt next to the doctor's rocking chair and looked into her eyes. "We will see each other again. Promise me at least that much. We *will* see each other again."

112

Bohnesy nodded. Ari lifted her cup and put it to her lips, and the doctor took a sip. "If the One Who Rules decides we should meet again, then we will meet."

Ari lowered the cup. "Now get out of here while you can," said Dr. Bohnes. "Get out. I mean it." She turned her face from Ari and gazed out the window.

Ari walked out of the sitting room, to the front entrance of the cottage. The boy Varto was standing there. He opened the door for her. Before Ari walked out she said, "You take good care of her. I want you to watch her every minute. If something bad happens to her while I'm gone —"

"Relax, mum," said the boy in an easy tone. "I know 'ow much you love 'er."

Ari nodded and walked out onto the porch. It was a downpour outside. Chase was standing under the roof of the porch, out of the rain. Ari raised the Royal Scepter over her head and thought about an umbrella — she concentrated on it, forming a picture in her mind. *I want an umbrella*, she thought. A moment later a wide magical glow formed over her head. She stepped out from under the porch and the rain bounced off the glow, keeping her dry.

The magic will find you, Dr. Bohnes had said. Ari knew in her heart that it was true.

"Let's go, Chase," Ari said. "It's time to fight the Shifter."

About the Author

Mary Stanton loves adventure. She has lived in Japan, Hawaii, and all over the United States. She has held many different jobs, including singing in a nightclub, working for an advertising agency, and writing for a TV cartoon series. Mary lives on a farm in upstate New York with some of the horses who inspire her to write adventure stories like the UNICORNS OF BALINOR.